# MISSING AMISH DAUGHTER

## A ROMANTIC SUSPENSE NOVELLA

### AMISH DETECTIVE BENUEL MILLER
### BOOK THREE

## RACHEL J. GOOD

This book is a work of fiction. Names, characters, places, and incidents are the product of the author's imagination or are used fictitiously. Any resemblance to actual events, locales, or persons, living or dead, is coincidental.

PRAYERFUL PRODUCTIVITY

Copyright © 2023 by Rachel J. Good

All Scripture from the *King James Version* of the *Holy Bible*

ISBN: 978-1-63888-027-0 (ebook)

978-1-63888-028-8 (print)

Printed in the USA

10 9 8 7 6 5 4 3 2 1

# CHAPTER 1

*I*f Mari Miller had known the dangers the day would bring, she'd have spent the whole morning on her knees instead of preparing breakfast. In the predawn darkness, the propane lamp just outside the kitchen doorway cast only a small circle of light around her as she slid a sausage and egg casserole into the oven.

Instead of rolling the light near her work surface, she'd left it in the living room to brighten her stepdaughter's way down the stairs. Mari hoped it would encourage Susanna to join her in preparing the meal.

Eleven-year-old Susanna had been a huge help when Mari first moved into the house after marrying Susanna's father, but over the past six months, Susanna had grown sulky and irritable. Each day with Benuel increased Mari's joy, and she hummed around the house as she took over the household chores, lightening Susanna's load. The poor girl had been doing all these jobs alone since her *mamm* had died when she was younger. Yet, the more Mari helped, the grumpier Susanna became. A dark cloud hung over her, and her moodiness dampened Mari's spirits.

Benuel's shuffling footsteps overhead erased her gloom. She closed her eyes and thanked God for this special man He'd brought into her life. The stairs creaked, and Mari fluttered into the living room to meet her husband as he descended, carefully feeling his way down each step. At the bottom, he turned toward her and opened his arms. She marveled at how, despite his loss of sight, he always knew exactly where she stood. God had blessed him with other keen senses, and Benuel had honed them as a detective.

Mari flew into his arms and melted against him. Here, in her husband's arms, she felt safe and protected. Twice, he'd saved her from near death. She cherished every moment they had together.

Something crashed overhead and shattered. Susanna's loud stomping poured icy water on Mari's ardor. She stepped out of Benuel's arms. They kept their embraces private.

A grumbling Susanna banged down the stairs. She glared at Mari, an expression her *daed* couldn't see, but amazingly, he sensed it.

"Apologize to Mari now," he commanded.

Susanna jerked back, a sour expression on her face. "I'm sorry, Mari." The words came out flat and sullen. "Will you forgive me?"

Benuel frowned, but before he could correct her, Mari laid a hand on his arm. She released her gritted teeth to say sweetly, "Of course I forgive you. Breakfast will be ready as soon as your *daed* and I tend the horses."

A storm cloud settled over Susanna's face. She brushed past Mari and her *daed* with a clipped, "I see."

"Susanna!"

Benuel's barked rebuke brought her to a stop.

"I'm sorry, *Daed*. I didn't mean to be rude." This time, she sounded genuinely apologetic. "It's just that I knocked my china bird from *Mamm* onto the floor, and—" Her words turned teary. "It broke."

"*Ach*, Susanna." Benuel turned from Mari to hug his *dochder*. "I know how much that meant to you."

So did Mari. Susanna treasured that bird. It had been the last gift her mother had given her. Mari's heart ached for her stepdaughter.

Susanna clung to her father, and he patted her back. Mari stood awkwardly nearby, wishing she could reach out and offer comfort, but Susanna would only jerk away.

After a few minutes, Benuel stepped back. "I know it's hard to lose that gift from your *mamm*, but remember, *dochder*, it was only made of clay. Your true treasure is in heaven."

Susanna pinched her lips together and straightened. Resolve tightened her face, but it didn't mask the grief in her eyes.

Once again, Mari longed to enfold Susanna in her arms. If only she could take away the pain.

Her stepdaughter's voice wobbled when she said, "I'll go get the broom."

"*Gut.*" Benuel smiled at her. "Mari and I will meet you for breakfast when we're done with the horses."

A brief storm of rage flashed across Susanna's expression. Then her shoulders slumped, and she plodded toward the pantry, but not before she shot Mari a look of pure hatred.

BENUEL, who'd been tucking his arm in Mari's so she could guide him over the rough ground outside, stiffened and lifted his head. He swiveled his head in Susanna's direction. The whirlwind of emotions emanating from his *dochder* confused and dismayed him. Losing a precious gift accounted for the sadness. Pain pierced his heart. Yet, when he'd held her, she'd remained rigid and gave off an air of wariness, even suspicion. She'd held back as if. . .

As if she didn't trust him. As if she didn't believe he cared. But why?

He and his *dochder* had been so close. They'd depended on each other in the dark days after her *mamm*'s death. They'd clung to each other more tightly, spent all their time together, and Susanna had needed daily reassurance he was still alive. If he were honest, he'd needed the same from her. They shared all their feelings and did everything together.

Susanna had understood his loneliness for a wife and urged him to date. He hadn't found anyone who interested him. Not until Mari. His *dochder* had pushed him toward Mari and encouraged their budding relationship. Susanna had been overjoyed when he and Mari married.

Those first few weeks, the three of them had bonded— doing chores together, sharing their joys and problems, reading the Bible together, playing games, running errands. Slowly, though, Susanna had pulled away, becoming more aloof as each day passed.

Now, waves of anger disturbed the air between them. Yet, despite Susanna's outer layer of simmering irritation, her footsteps and bowed shoulders sent off signals of deep heartbreak. *Jah*, she ached over losing her precious keepsake, but this grief went deeper. She seemed to be weighed down by a loss she couldn't bear.

What wasn't she telling him? What secret was she hiding?

Had he been so caught up with his brand-new relationship with Mari he'd been neglecting Susanna? Benuel promised himself he'd rectify that today when she came home from school. As much as he loved having Mari's help in his secondhand shop, perhaps getting

Susanna alone would encourage her to confide what was wrong.

After Susanna stomped up the stairs with the broom, Benuel took Mari's arm. "I'm sorry," he whispered. "I wish I knew why she's been acting so prickly."

"It's all right." Mari's gentle voice soothed him. She opened the back door and led him toward the barn. "I'm sure she'll come around. Let's just give her some time."

"But it's been months. You've been nothing but kind." It ripped him up inside that his sweet Mari was being hurt.

She moved closer to him. "I've been praying. We just need to trust the Lord."

Her nearness, her softness stirred a tenderness in him. He appreciated her caring, her acceptance, her wisdom. Love flooded through him, overflowing with each step they took. Benuel longed to embrace her, kiss her right there on the driveway, but his *Englisch* neighbor might be heading out to tend to his cows. And the cars growling past on the lane below checked his impulse.

Before they separated for chores, Benuel hesitated. "I've been thinking. . ." He didn't want to hurt Mari's feelings. He started again. "As much as I want you around every second of the day, it wonders me if I should spend time alone with Susanna in the shop this afternoon."

"That's a good idea. I'll miss you, but we have all day together."

Not quite true. They both had work to do. Still, Mari stopped in as often as she could to help. Once she finished her household chores, she brought quilting or mending to the store so they could be together in the afternoons before she started supper. She kept busy with her needlework whenever she wasn't helping customers or *redding* up the shop.

"*Danke* for being so understanding." When Mari passed

5

RACHEL J. GOOD

him to head into the next stall, Benuel reached out and drew her into his arms. "I'm so grateful God brought you into my life."

"Me too." She stood on tiptoe to press her lips to his.

Benuel's heart expanded in his chest until it ached. How blessed he was to have her in his life! God had given him a precious treasure.

Susanna clomped into the barn.

Mari and Benuel jumped apart and hastily returned to the horses.

"Aren't you done yet?" Susanna's snarky attitude grated on Benuel's nerves.

"That's enough," he snapped, then regretted his harshness. *A soft answer turneth away wrath.* Praying for control over his temper, he said in more measured tones, "I want you to ask your question again. This time respectfully."

Susanna heaved a sigh. "Do. . . you. . . need. . . help?" She laced her monotone words with sulkiness.

"That was a start. Try it again without the attitude."

"All you do is criticize me." Susanna turned and ran from the barn.

Benuel pivoted to go after her, but Mari held onto his arm.

"Give her a little time to calm down. Maybe she'll regret acting this way and come back to apologize."

Benuel wasn't so sure. If it had been six months ago, he had no doubt she'd turn around and rush back to beg for forgiveness. But back then, she'd never have acted like this.

What was wrong with her? She'd always been loving and caring. He'd heard girls sometimes grew moody as they became teenagers, but his senses warned him this ran deeper.

Susanna resented Mari, but Benuel had no idea why. Mari had been nothing but kind and gentle with his

6

daughter, and Susanna and Mari had gotten along so well before the wedding. And even during the first few months afterward. Yet, the more Mari did for Susanna, the more helpful Mari became, the grouchier Susanna grew.

His lovely *dochder* had turned *mürrisch*. Even worse, bitterness churned beneath the surface. Benuel sensed a storm brewing. A storm he could do nothing to stop.

# CHAPTER 2

*S*usanna flew out of the house after breakfast, rage gripping her insides in a tight vise, squeezing her heart until her whole chest burned. With shaking fingers, she hitched her pony to the cart. Ignoring her father's lifelong warnings about treating horses gently, she clucked until Peach galloped. The cart, which could easily tip at that speed, rocked violently. But she didn't care. Her irritation at Mari made her reckless.

She'd left the house without offering to help with dishes. It didn't matter. Mari would insist on doing them herself. She always did. Mari had taken over everything. Not that Susanna minded getting out of dishwashing, but what bothered her was the way Mari had edged Susanna out of everything—cooking, household chores, waiting on customers in the store. Even out of *Daed*'s life.

Once, he'd depended on her for everything. Now, he had Mari. He had no need of his *dochder*'s arm to guide him. No need of her reminders to eat his supper. No need of her company at meals or her conversations in the evening. No need of her at all.

And Susanna had no time alone with him. No quiet Bible readings together. No chats about her school and friends. No picnics in the meadow. No quiet drives on back roads to listen to birds and smell the flowers and ripening crops. No laughing over games or cards in the evenings.

They still did all those things. Except instead of being just the two of them, everything—every single minute—included Mari. When *Daed* needed a hand, he reached for Mari. When he wanted to share stories about his day, he directed them to Mari. When he complimented a meal, Mari had made it.

*Mari, Mari, Mari* filled his conversation from the moment he woke until he fell into bed at night. Rather than turning to Susanna, who had been his constant companion and helper after *Mamm* died, he relied on his new wife.

*Why did I encourage him to court her? I thought she was so sweet. But she's turned into the wicked stepmother from Englisch fairy tales.*

Susanna's conscience pricked her. *Did Mari really change? Or is my jealousy of her time with Daed blinding me to her good points? Is this the devil tempting me?*

Susanna's conscience warned her to confess her anger and envy. To get right with God and Mari. Susanna pushed away that possibility, much too upset to forgive or apologize. Feeling furious at Mari felt better.

Due to her early start and her driving speed, Susanna arrived at school long before the other scholars. Even before Teacher Rose. The deserted schoolyard pointed up Susanna's loneliness. She'd been pushed out of her *daed*'s life. And she'd been walling herself off from her friends. Everyone praised her stepmother. So kind. So loving. So thoughtful. That isolated Susanna even more. She had no one who'd listen and understand.

Once, she'd agreed with all those compliments about Mari. Now hearing them drove sharp nail points into her already bloodied heart. Susanna could barely look at her stepmother. All the positives about Mari could never outweigh everything she'd taken away.

Alone in the schoolyard, Susanna pulled Peach to a stop. She hopped from the cart and ran a hand over the slick wetness of her pony's coat.

"I'm so sorry, Peach." She threw her arms around her pony's neck. "I never should have done this to you."

Peach was all lathered up, but Susanna had nothing to sop up the sweat. Nothing except the quilted lap blanket Mari had made to keep Susanna warm on chilly days. *Gut!* That was a fitting use for anything Mari's hands had touched.

"I'm not mad at you, Peach." Tears burned behind Susanna's eyes as she rubbed down her pony. "I didn't mean to hurt you."

All the *I'm sorry*s welling up inside of her spilled from her eyes and down her cheeks. She had so much to be sorry about. So much she'd lost. So much she regretted. But even as her heart softened, another part of her hardened toward Mari. The woman who'd taken everything Susanna needed and wanted. The woman who'd cut Susanna off from her *daed*.

Her school day passed in a blur. Teacher Rose smiled and patted Susanna's arm as she hung around the classroom after school ended, reluctant to leave. What was the point of heading home? Mari would be working in the store.

"It's nice you have more time for yourself now that your *daed* has married." Delight lit Teacher Rose's face, and soft, crinkly lines appeared beside her eyes.

Susanna ducked her head and mumbled a noncommittal response. She couldn't burst out with her complaints. Nobody would understand. Especially not Teacher Rose, who taught them to be thankful in all things.

Shuffling her feet, Susanna donned her safety vest and headed for the door of the schoolroom. "I'd better go. *Daed* might still need me." Her face burned at the lie. Her father didn't need her. And he never would. Not as long as he had Mari.

Outside, Susanna moseyed along, kicking at fallen leaves in the parking lot until the other scholars had all gone home. If she dawdled long enough, maybe she'd arrive home after *Daed* had closed the shop for supper. Then she wouldn't have to see Mari chatting with customers or, even worse, smiling at *Daed* in that special way she had—as if he was the most important person in the world. A smile that left Susanna out in the cold.

"Run along, Susanna," Teacher Rose said behind her.

Susanna jumped. She'd been so lost in thought, she'd lost track of where she was.

The teacher waited until Susanna harnessed Peach to the pony cart before hitching up her own horse. Then Teacher Rose followed Susanna down the long, winding dirt path to the road. Rose waved as she turned one way and Susanna turned the other.

As soon as Teacher Rose's horse trotted out of sight, Susanna turned her pony cart around and headed back to the school. After looping Peach's reins around one of the hitching posts at the edge of the schoolyard, Susanna plopped onto on a swing and drifted idly back and forth, too discouraged to even bother pumping her feet.

She'd wait until almost suppertime before she headed home. Would they even care she hadn't come back from school? Or would they be too wrapped up in each other to notice?

The sun sank lower, but even the beauty of lavender, rose, and peach streaking the sky didn't lift Susanna's spirits the way it usually did.

*Mamm* always thanked God for painting heavenly pictures. Sunsets, sunrises, and starry skies had been times of thanksgiving. Who knew *Mamm* would enjoy so few of them? Why had God taken her so young?

And now He'd taken *Daed* too. *Daed* was still alive, but so far away, he might as well be in heaven.

Susanna shivered. As dusk fell, the air grew chillier. She'd used the small quilt to rub down Peach and had nothing to wrap around herself. Maybe she should head home before she caught a chill.

Reluctantly, she untied Peach and started down the hill. Fall days were much too short. She didn't want to get home before supper, but *Daed* had drummed it into her never to drive the pony cart at night. The small cart was hard to see in daylight. After dark, though, *Englisch* boys revved loud cars and trucks, speeding and racing on the country roads. They raced so fast they left tire tracks and roadkill in their wake. She didn't need to be one of their victims.

If she didn't make it home before dark, *Daed* would take away her privilege of driving to school. That meant more than an hour's walk each way. Or even worse, because it stayed so dark in the mornings, he might insist on Mari driving her to school. Most Amish parents would think nothing of letting their children walk before the sun rose. But because a drunk driver had veered into *daed*'s younger sister as she walked to school in the early morning darkness and crippled her, *Daed* made sure Susanna never walked in the dark.

As she passed the thickest part of the woods, an acrid odor filled the air, choking her.

What was that strange smell?

She'd never noticed it during the day while she was at school. Definitely not someone burning leaves. Besides, nobody would burn leaves deep in the woods. Were the trees on fire? *Neh*, that was not wood smoke. These fumes stung her eyes.

Susanna sniffed, trying not to draw in too much air at one time. It smelled like. . . like rotten eggs. Her stomach churned, making her want to hold her breath.

One summer, when she was five, she'd been playing in at the park and found a leftover Easter egg hidden in the base of a tree. The marbled colors fascinated her, so she took it home as a keepsake. But it had rolled off her dresser and splattered on the floor. *Ach!* The stink of it! And poor *daed* with his sensitive nose had made her scrub the wooden floor over and over until he could no longer smell a trace of it.

*Jah*, rotten eggs. The odor choked her.

*Meow. . . Meow. . .*

The plaintive mewl tore at Susanna's heart. She pulled on the reins to stop her pony.

A tiny white kitten nosed in the brown fallen leaves. *Poor little thing!*

Where was its mother? The baby sounded hungry and scared.

Susanna eased out of the pony cart, but her movements frightened the kitten. It scampered off—a tiny snowball in the now almost dark woods. She had to find it and make sure it found its mother.

She tied Peach to a nearby pine tree and hurried off after the kitten.

"Snowball," she called softly as the dark woods closed around her, blocking out the last of the daylight.

# CHAPTER 3

*a*s autumn leaves skipped on the breeze, the late afternoon sky outside the window darkened. Mari glanced anxiously at the battery-powered clock on the kitchen wall. Susanna should be home from school by now.

Mari's eyes stung. She was unsure if the moisture came from the onion she was chopping for their supper stew or because of Susanna's coldness and loathing this morning.

Before Mari had married Benuel in the spring, Susanna had been cheerful, cooperative, and supportive of her father's relationship and the upcoming wedding. But now that Mari had moved into their home, Susanna had grown sullen and uncooperative. The harder Mari tried to reach her stepdaughter, the more distant Susanna became.

*Lord, please show me how to reach her and let her know I love her.*

Mari's knife clunked a steady rhythm of *chop, chop, chop* that didn't match the rapid, uneven patter of her heart. Dusk had fallen. Susanna should have been home long before this. Benuel insisted Susanna never walk or drive after dark. Was she deliberately defying the rules?

Hooves thundered up the driveway. Mari clenched her

fists. Benuel had warned Susanna several times recently about driving the cart too fast. Now, he'd probably have to punish her for disobedience, adding to Susanna's hostility.

Mari sighed, wiped her hands on a dishtowel, and headed for the door, unsure what she could do to diffuse the situation. Still, she had to try.

Benuel rarely got upset or angry, but he would never allow his daughter to mistreat her pony. Susanna had always been gentle around animals. This behavior was so out of character.

In front of the house, the door to Benuel's secondhand shop banged open. Mari raced toward her husband. He could pick his way carefully across the parking lot to the driveway, but she sensed his impatience.

"I'm coming," she called.

He stopped and waited for her. "*Danke.*"

Breathless, she stopped in front of him, her heart clenching at the anguish on his face.

"What are we going to do about her?" he burst out. "I've prayed and prayed for guidance, but she disobeys every rule. And the way she treats you. . ." His voice broke.

"Don't worry about me," Mari assured him. She took his arm, and they hurried across the parking lot together.

"I can't help worrying. I want my daughter to love you the way I do—with a whole heart."

Mari squeezed his arm as her joy overflowed. She'd never dreamed she'd be married to such a wonderful man. A man who cherished her. A man who protected and cared for her. A man who'd risked his life to save her.

"Give Susanna time to get used to me. This is a whole new experience for her."

"Before we married, she insisted she couldn't wait to have a new *mamm*. Yet, she's been so rude and unkind to you." Benuel's heartbreak came across in his words.

15

"Perhaps in time. . ."

"I don't want you to have to endure this. I want her to change now."

They rushed up the inclined driveway toward the barn.

Peach had come to a sudden stop by the barn door, flanks heaving.

Mari gasped.

Benuel's fingers dug into her arm. "What's wrong?"

But Mari couldn't answer. The pony cart lay on the gravel drive. Overturned and empty.

Mari swiveled her head to scan the driveway, the yard, the porch. No Susanna. The lathered-up pony had galloped up the driveway, dragging only a pony cart behind.

Where was Susanna? Had she gotten out on the road and sent Peach careening up the driveway to scare them? It wouldn't be the first time she'd tried a mean trick. Mari half expected Susanna to stroll up to them, a mocking expression on her face.

But her stepdaughter was nowhere in sight.

"Tell me," Benuel commanded.

"The. . .the cart's empty. And it's overturned." Mari's voice shook.

Benuel pulled free, and without waiting for her guidance, jogged toward the pony.

"Be careful," Mari warned. She hurried after him, praying he wouldn't trip.

When he reached Peach, Benuel ran his hands expertly over the pony, checking for injuries. Thank the Lord, she had none that he could detect. Rapidly, he felt along the shaft and squatted beside the upturned cart.

Mari knelt beside him.

"Susanna's not in the driveway or road?" Benuel righted the cart, felt the wheels.

"*Neh*, I checked."

He stood. "She must have fallen out."

Although he spoke in his usual calm manner, tension oozed from his words.

"Can you ready the buggy while I unhitch Peach and put her in her stall? He undid the traces and shafts to unhook her from the cart and took the pony to the barn.

Mari sprinted ahead of him to open the doors. While Benuel hustled Peach carefully toward her stall, she grabbed the DeWalt light they kept hanging in the barn and set it in the buggy. With trembling hands, she backed the buggy into the driveway and led Blossom from her stall. Mari rarely wished for a car, but she did now. They needed to hurry.

What had happened to Susanna? Suppose she lay in the road and a speeding car didn't see her? What if she'd been thrown from the cart and lay badly hurt in the fields? Or—

*Stop it!* Taking a deep breath, Mari breathed deeply to calm her racing mind. God was in control. They had to accept His will. Whatever the Lord had planned for her— and Susanna and Benuel—was for the best. Mari had to trust the Lord. But she could ask Him for help.

*Please, Lord, if it's Your will, keep Susanna safe and help us find her.*

~

BENUEL SLID his feet along the barn floor, searching for obstacles to trip him up. He moved as quickly as he could, leading Peach and praying for his daughter's safety. He felt for the stall latch, lifted it, and urged the pony inside. His hands slid rapidly over the harness in his usual practiced pattern to free the pony. But as he lifted the bridle to remove it, he halted in midair. Something seemed off. He balanced it on his hand. It was lighter than usual.

He'd memorized every nuance of the equipment. Other

people might not notice a few ounces of difference in the weight, but he did. He probed every inch of the leather. As he fingered the reins, a chill swept down his spine. The reins were much too short and ended in jagged edges. They'd been torn loose.

A splinter jabbed Benuel's finger, drawing a spot of blood. He sucked at the tiny wound for a moment, then felt around cautiously for the source of his pain. A small shard of wood had lodged in the end of one rein. Benuel lifted the tiny sliver to his nose.

*Pine resin.*

Susanna had tied Peach to a tree. Why hadn't she hooked the pony to the hitching post at school? And why had Peach had broken free? Had something frightened her?

A snake? An animal? From time to time, bears had been spotted in the woods around here. Suppose whatever scared the pony had attacked Susanna?

Peach shied at gunshots. Hunters often trespassed in the woods below the school grounds. Maybe shots had ricocheted near the pony, terrifying her. Suppose a bullet had gone wild and hit his daughter, knocking her off the cart? She could be bleeding to death on the ground somewhere.

Benuel reined in his thoughts. Just because the pony had been spooked by an animal or a bullet, it didn't mean Susanna had been hurt. Perhaps she hadn't been in the cart and she'd only been stranded when Peach took off. She might still be walking home.

Benuel felt his way outside. "Mari?" he called.

"Over here."

He picked his way carefully over the gravel in the direction of his wife's voice and the jingle of metal buckles.

"Peach broke free."

Mari stiffened. "She did?"

The slight quaver in her voice and the tension emanating

from her as he set a hand on her shoulder told Benuel she was as worried as he was. They had to hurry and find Susanna.

His fingers flew as he helped Mari finish hitching up Blossom. And his prayers raced upward even more rapidly.

*Please, Lord, keep my little girl safe. Don't let her end up like my sister. Please help us find her. Direct our path and lead us to her. Show us where to go.*

In addition to being hit by a bullet, Susanna could have fallen from the cart as she rode. His mind filled with pictures of his *dochder* crushed and broken at the side of the road.

Mari hopped into the driver's seat, and he climbed in beside her.

"What do you think happened?" she asked, her voice tremulous.

Benuel reached for her hand. She was shaking. His own heart pounded out a staccato rhythm of worry and fear.

"It'll be all right," he assured her. "I've been praying."

"I have too." But her words sounded hesitant and unsure. Then she fell silent.

*Jah*, he'd been begging the Lord for guidance and to keep Susanna safe, but what if that wasn't God's will for them? What if the Lord planned to take Susanna? Or to leave her bedridden for life like his sister Jessica.

As the buggy bumped down the driveway, Benuel wrestled with that possibility. Could he give his *dochder* to the Lord? How would they care for her if she could never walk again? Even worse, what if the Lord chose to take her? How could he live without her? What if he never talked to her again? Never held her in his arms?

Why hadn't he told her how much he loved her this morning? His last conversation with her had been filled with criticism and scolding. If only he could go back and redo that morning. He'd be more understanding of her loss of the china bird. After all, it was the last gift from her *mamm*. He'd have spent more time with her, knowing he might never speak to her again.

The buggy wheels clattered along the road, and Mari clicked, signaling Blossom to pick up speed. The horse broke into a trot, and Benuel rued his inability to see. He disliked being useless.

"Wait!" he shouted.

Mari tugged on the reins to slow the horse.

"What if Susanna's lying along the road here? We might race past and miss her."

"You're right." Mari pulled Blossom to a stop and glanced around. "It's also possible Susanna's playing a joke, and she's hiding in the trees laughing at us."

Benuel hadn't thought of that. Susanna did like to tease. But would she do something this cruel? His daughter had never had a mean streak. Lately, though. . .

Lifting the DeWalt, Mari twisted in the driver's seat to check in all directions. She kept Blossom to a plodding pace, stopping often to shine the light into trees, bushes, and fields alongside the road.

"I wish I could help you look for her," he burst out.

"It's all right. I can do it. I'm just happy you're here with me. You always calm me." She set down the lantern and entwined her fingers with his.

He squeezed hers gently. God had given him a wonderful helpmeet. "I'm so glad I married you. I was just thinking that if something had happened to Susanna before we were together, I couldn't have searched for her right away."

"I'm happy I can do something for you after all you've done for me. And you never know. We may need your skills too."

That thought chilled Benuel.

# CHAPTER 4

*T*hey painstakingly covered the miles to the schoolhouse. Beside Benuel, Mari turned from side to side, occasionally stopping to hop out and check the shadows. Benuel railed at being so useless. All he could do was pray.

He sent up petition after petition until they reached the narrow, rutted lane up the hill to the schoolhouse.

*Please, Lord, help us find her.*

Benuel sensed the change in atmosphere as they entered the wooded area. Besides the usual aroma of pine drifting through his window, he noticed a strange scent coming from the woods to his left. Very faintly in the distance, the air reeked of cat urine and. . . Was that sulphur?

He sat forward in his seat. "Do you smell that?"

Mari slowed the buggy even more. She sniffed. Air movements told him she was swiveling her head from side to side. "Smell what?"

"That sharp stink." It burned his sensitive nostrils.

She drew in several deep breaths as Blossom picked her

way up the hill. "*Neh*, I don't smell anything. What is it? Not fire, I hope."

"Nothing like that. It's hard to describe. I remember cleaning my cat's litter box years ago. It's something like that. But it's mixed with the odor of sulphur. Like rotten eggs."

"But why would the woods smell like that?"

Mari sounded as puzzled as Benuel felt. He'd love to solve this mystery, but first, they needed to find Susanna.

Despite the stench drifting their way, he stuck his head out the window. "You see anything?"

"*Neh*. Not any sign of Susanna. And nothing to account for that odor you described."

By the smooth flatness after the rutted dirt lane, they'd reached the school playground. The caustic air burned his eyes and throat.

As soon as Mari steered Blossom toward the hitching post and stopped, Benuel hopped out. Using the side of the buggy and the shafts and pony as guides, he reached the post at the same time as Mari. He took the reins from her hands, lingering a moment to give her a grateful squeeze, and secured the reins. He wanted to do something, anything, to be useful.

"Now what?" she asked, her voice tremulous.

"We examine every inch of this playground."

WITH A HEAVY HEART, Mari offered Benuel her arm and held the DeWalt high, illuminating the ground to keep them both from tripping. Together, they traversed the blacktop. Benuel ran his hands over the swings and stopped on the second one.

"I think she was here not long ago."

"How do you know?"

He shrugged. "I just sense her presence."

While he stood there, concentrating, probably hoping and praying for a clue to where Susanna had gone next, Mari hurried over to the schoolhouse and tried the door.

"It's locked," she called, but she banged on it anyway. "Susanna? Susanna? Are you in there?"

No answer.

Mari shone the light into the windows, but the building appeared empty. She continued calling Susanna name as she returned to Benuel's side.

"Find anything?"

He shook his head. Mari's spirits plummeted.

*LORD, show us where to go next*, Benuel prayed.

Despite his petition, panic filled his chest. Suppose she'd been hit by a car and was lying in the hospital. Or the morgue. If the police came to the house to tell them, someone should be there.

Ever since Mari's run-in with her crazed twin sister on their wedding day, Benuel had kept a cell phone on him. The main numbers he had programmed into it were his contacts at the FBI. They wouldn't get involved with a missing girl unless she'd been kidnapped and taken over state lines, but he pulled out the phone.

"I'm going to call Burkey." Their Mennonite neighbor would help.

Mari pressed close to him. "Good idea."

A few minutes later, Benuel had explained the situation and arranged for Burkey to stay at their house in case law enforcement arrived. Burkey also offered to contact the bishop and call area hospitals to see if Susanna had been admitted.

Grateful for his assistance, Benuel thanked him multiple times before hanging up. Then he hugged Mari, drawing strength and comfort from her closeness.

"We'll find her," she whispered. "Once the bishop knows we're here, everyone in the *g'may* will rush up here and form search parties."

Benuel nodded. *Jah*, they'd have plenty of help. But a crowd of people might trample clues. "Mari, quick. Take me to the edge of the asphalt. I want to see if I can find any signs of Susanna before anyone arrives."

~

MARI LED him to the spot where the dirt road began, and Benuel squatted, running his hands over the ground.

"What are you doing?" she asked.

"Checking the wheel ruts." He frowned in concentration. "These deeper ones are from buggies. Some of them crisscross over top of others, making it hard to tell them apart."

Mari marveled at her husband's detective skills. She never would have thought to check wheel tracks. She knelt near him and cast the light on the soft, damp earth.

"See these shallower indentations? They're from a pony cart. And these very light ones? Those are scooters. The wide ones are tire tracks from a car or truck. And look at the hoof prints."

Now that Benuel had pointed them out, Mari could see the patterns. Between all the buggy wheel marks, she spotted the distinct hoof prints. Most children walked or rode scooters, so scattered footprint and scooter tracks wove in and out over the tire tracks.

Tire tracks?

"Probably teens coming up here to party or smooch."

"*Jah.*" It would be a secluded spot for getting into trouble.

Although the tire imprints lay below the other tracks, it started Mari worrying. What if some of those teens had come up here and found Susanna alone? Would they hurt her?

She shook off the worrisome images. *Mamm* had always taught her that worry meant they weren't trusting God.

As Mari struggled to turn all her fearful thoughts over to God, Benuel distracted her by gesturing to the freshest marks he'd been touching. "These tracks are the most recent. They're ours." He sighed. "I wish we'd thought to leave the buggy down by the road. We rolled right over clues."

"I'm sorry." Mari's only thought had been getting to Susanna as soon as possible.

Benuel shot her a loving smile. "I didn't think about it either. And we didn't mess up all the tracks. These must be from Teacher Rose's buggy."

By raising the lantern, Mari could follow that trail with her eyes. Their own buggy tracks cut into Rose's tracks in several places.

"These are the most recent traces of a pony cart. They must be Susanna's."

"*Jah.*" For a few yards they wavered back and forth as if Susanna had been nervous or unsteady.

After Benuel traced them with his fingers, he rocked back on his haunches and stroked his beard. "Why wasn't she driving straight? Had something frightened her? Maybe she was glancing behind her?"

Her husband's words made sense. "But what would she be afraid of?" Mari asked him.

"An animal? Some rowdy *Englisch* teens planning to party? Whatever it was, Teacher Rose was still here. See how her buggy tracks cut over Susanna's?"

Mari's mind conjured up other more dangerous possibilities. "What if those tracks aren't Rose's?"

"Who in the community would do Susanna harm?" Yet, for some reason, Benuel's mind stayed stuck on *youngie*. Could Amish teens have chased Susanna downhill? But who? And why? And what happened to her after that?

He didn't voice those concerns to Mari. They seemed too farfetched.

Benuel's phone buzzed. He answered and mouthed to Mari, "Teacher Rose." He put her on speaker so his wife could hear.

"As soon as I heard Susanna's missing, I rushed right to the phone shanty to call you. The bishop's organizing search parties. They'll be heading to the schoolhouse soon."

"*Danke.* Can you tell me anything about what Susanna did after school today?"

Rose hesitated. "You know, she didn't pay attention well in class today. Usually, she's the first to answer, but she acted distracted. Moody. Sad. And maybe angry?" She paused. "Did anything happen this morning at home? I didn't notice any trouble at school, although she didn't chatter with her friends the way she normally does."

Benuel squeezed his eyes shut. He regretted his harshness with his *dochder*. "Susanna broke a china bird, the last present her *mamm* ever gave her." His voice went thick as he struggled to speak.

"*Ach*, I'm so sorry. That might be why she looked as if she wanted to cry several times today. I was worried about her."

Rose's words pierced him. He'd been so caught up in Mari and, if he were honest, upset about Susanna interrupting their embrace. He should have paid more attention to his little girl.

Mari moved closer and linked her arm through his. He smiled at her, grateful she understood his need for comfort.

But Rose's observations about the morning weren't helping them locate Susanna now. If she'd been upset and run away, which Rose seemed to be implying, Susanna could be cold, hungry, lost, or in great danger. They needed to find her.

Benuel interrupted Rose's concerns about Susanna staying aloof from her friends at recess. "Can you tell me when she left school at the end of the day?"

Rose grew quiet. "That was odd, now that you mention it. I stayed almost an hour later to grade some essays and work on plans for tomorrow. When I came out, Susanna hadn't put on her safety vest or hitched up her pony cart."

"She hadn't?" His *dochder* had strict instructions to come straight home. And she'd always been the first one out of the schoolyard because she hurried home to help in the store.

Guilt niggled at Benuel. Now that Mari worked with him, Susanna didn't have a reason to rush home. Half the time, when she arrived at the house after school, she didn't even bother coming to the shop at all. Had she been feeling left out?

Teacher Rose chattered on, but Benuel missed what she'd said. He didn't want to ask her to repeat it. He concentrated on what she was saying now.

"Anyway, I waited until she put on her vest and got in the pony cart to hitch up my horse. Then I followed her down the lane and to the street. I waved to her as we each turned opposite ways on the street."

"So, she reached the road?"

"*Jah*, we both did. And she headed toward home."

"*Danke* for letting me know."

"Of course. I'll be coming out there to help soon. The bishop wants to use the schoolhouse as a base for the search

27

parties. *Mamm* and my sisters are gathering food and supplies."

Benuel swallowed hard. Rose made it sound as if this would be a long operation. As if his *dochder* might be missing for days rather than hours. The heaviness inside expanded until his whole chest hurt.

"And we're all praying," Rose added.

"*Danke.*" Benuel whispered his own prayers after he hung up.

"I guess we need to start where Rose last saw Susanna. At the turnoff by the main road." *And hope there wasn't an accident.*

Where was his *dochder*? What had happened to her?

# CHAPTER 5

Once she tied Peach securely, Susanna followed the tiny kitten deeper into the trees. That horrible stink choked her, burning her lungs. No moon lit her path, and dead leaves crunched underfoot.

She'd never been frightened of the darkness before, but prickles of unease ran down her spine. All around her, twigs stuck out like skeleton fingers, eager to grab her. The breeze bounced them so they appeared to be beckoning her, urging her to come closer—into a trap.

A strong wind whipped them into a frenzy, rattling them like bones. Overhead, branches twisted and twined together, blotting out the sky the farther she went, turning the gaps between the trees into shadowy, cavernous shapes. Like mouths waiting to swallow her up.

Something rustled the bushes nearby. The sharp crack of branches made her freeze. What would be in these woods at night?

Foxes? Bears?

Susanna could barely breathe. The spit in her mouth dried.

Bears had been spotted around here recently. An *Englischer* who lived alone in a cabin several miles down the road had startled a black bear rummaging through his trash can. That bear must live in these woods.

If one bear had a den around here, there must be more. They'd have families. What if a whole pack of them surrounded her?

Bears were strong and fast and deadly. People said never to run from them. Susanna wouldn't have any choice about following that advice. She was too petrified to move.

Her heart pounded so hard she could barely draw in a breath. *Daed!* She wanted her *daed*! She needed him.

If a bear ate her, he'd never know what happened to her.

*Would he miss me? Or would he and Mari be glad to be alone together without me?*

The rustling stopped. Had it been an animal? Or only the wind?

Susanna's eyes burned. From backed-up tears? Or from that yucky smell?

*Hoo-hoo. . .*

She jumped. Her heart raced even faster. That sound had come from a nearby tree.

*The kitten!* Would that owl swoop down and scoop the baby kitten into its sharp claws?

*Hoo-hoo. . .*

Something small skittered just ahead of her. The kitten? Would it know to hide?

She had to protect it, keep it safe.

Susanna stepped softly in that direction. As she moved deeper into the woods, her eyes adjusted to the dark. But here, trees grew so close together they cast deep shadows. Bushes poked out prickly, tangled thorns, scratching her arms.

*Turn around*, a still, small voice in her head warned her. *Turn around.*

But Susanna's stubbornness kept her inching ahead. She had to save that kitten.

A small smear of white on the ground ahead crept forward. Praying it was the kitten, Susanna pounced for it. It scuttled away.

"I don't want to hurt you. Please, kitten, let me help you," she whispered, her voice quavering.

Susanna bunched up her skirt and crawled into the bushes after it slowly, trying not to appear threatening. Her knees squished through slimy, decaying leaves. Slippery and ickiness oozed around her legs. She shivered. Sharp stones jabbed her. She kept going. She wouldn't give up until she'd rescued the kitten.

The white blur shifted direction, and Susanna stood and trailed it. She edged forward until she drew near enough. Slowly, silently, she reached out and captured the ball of fluff.

The kitten squirmed in her hands. Susanna rose, cuddling it close to her chest.

*Hoo-hoo. . .*

She hunched her body over the tiny baby. Would the owl swoop down and snatch the kitty from her arms? Would the hungry bird attack her?

Susanna imagined the talons digging into her head, tangling in her hair. A small cry escaped her lips.

*Please, Lord, keep me and Snowball safe from that owl.*

She had to get out of here. "I won't let anything hurt you," she promised the wriggling baby cat as she stroked its matted fur.

But she hadn't watched what direction she'd gone as she chased Snowball. Susanna turned in every direction. Nothing looked familiar. Which way was out?

Why hadn't she paid attention? *Daed* had taught her how to use all her senses. She'd never be as good as he was because she relied so much on her sight. But she could try. Her sight wasn't much use in this darkness.

A loud beating of wings startled her. The owl swished past, its powerful feathers throbbing the air above her.

Terrified, Susanna whirled around and crouched. She shielded Snowball, exposing her back to the predator.

But the owl glided over her. Behind her, scuffling and squeaking revealed it had captured its prey. Susanna stayed huddled and trembling until the flapping of mighty wings lifted the bird to the treetops. Then, she stood shakily.

Holding the kitten, Susanna returned to studying the woods. The treetops rustled as she rotated in a tight circle. The trees and bushes appeared identical in every direction. But the smell. That stink had grown stronger and stronger the deeper she went into the woods.

"*Danke, Daed,*" she murmured. If it weren't for his lessons, she might not have thought about that.

All she had to do was walk in any direction, keeping track of that horrid odor. If it lessened, she was headed out of the woods. If it stayed the same, she was moving to the left or right. If it grew worse, she was walking in the wrong direction.

For the first time that night, she had hope. With the kitten in her arms, she stepped forward confidently, sniffing the air. She had to forge ahead quite a distance before she could assure herself she was going in the wrong direction. Not only had the stink increased, but her eyes stung more.

Despite the disgusting odor, Susanna smiled. She only had to turn the other way to get out of these woods.

She bent her head and touched her lips to the kitten's fuzzy ears. "We did it, Snowball," she whispered.

Straightening her shoulders, she faced the opposite direction. "I'll have your out of here in no time, little one."

Before she could take a step, loud thrashing came from behind her. Something huge crashed through the bushes. A bear. Nothing else could be that big.

She should run, but her feet stuck to the ground. Her mind raced. Maybe if she made no sound, the creature wouldn't know they were here.

Who was she fooling?

Animals could detect scents. And she and the kitty probably smelled like a delicious meal to a hungry bear. Susanna braced herself for the attack.

A huge hairy paw clamped over her mouth and dragged her backward.

# CHAPTER 6

"*L*et's walk," Benuel suggested. "That way we won't mess up any tracks." He doubted they'd need them if Susanna had reached the road, but he'd preserve them anyway. Things that seemed unimportant often ended up providing vital clues later.

He encouraged his wife to walk along the edge of the lane, and they shuffled through a carpet of damp leaves. The sulphury odor grew stronger partway down the hill. It burned and stung his nostrils.

"Where can that chemical smell be coming from?" he wondered aloud. "We have no homes or businesses nearby." The closest factory was ten miles in the opposite direction, and the woods extended for several miles to his right. Except for the schoolhouse, there were no buildings on this side of the mountain top.

Underneath the sharp, biting note, a lighter scent teased his nose. Pine and spruce. He stopped abruptly.

"Is something wrong?" Mari sounded fearful.

"Wait a second." He called to mind the land farther

down the hill. "Mari," he asked urgently, "can you think of any place with pine trees after we get to the road?"

Mari stayed silent for a moment, then her hand swept past him to the right. "This whole side of the road has pines until you reach the Esh farm."

"But Teacher Rose would head home that way. What about Susanna? She'd turn left."

"*Jah.* Only a few oak trees grow along here. Miller's farmland stretches along this road on the right. And from there it's mainly farms and cattle pastures. After that, Schrock's Dairy takes up most of the land until you reach the turn for our road."

She'd said "*our* road." Despite Benuel's fear over his *dochder*'s disappearance, his heart leapt a little. Mari considered the road *their road* now. She'd made herself at home. He'd worried she might miss her *aenti*'s place.

He slipped his arm from hers so he could pull her close. They'd become not only husband and wife, but a team. Two had become one. His heart pounded as she melted against him. So soft and gentle in his arms.

"I'm so glad you're my wife." Doubly so after he'd almost lost her to her evil twin's plots.

She stood on tiptoe to kiss his cheek. "And I'm so glad you're my husband."

"I'm not too much of a burden?" He always worried about that.

"A burden? Never. I can't live without you." She laid her head against his shoulder, making him feel strong and needed.

As soon as they found Susanna, he would show her how much he needed and wanted her. But right now, they had to find his missing *dochder*. Benuel slipped his arm from around his precious wife and reached into his pocket to finger the sliver. He pulled it out and sniffed it.

"What's that?" Mari asked.

He took her palm and set the splinter on it. "I found this stuck in Peach's reins." The only clue he had to Susanna's disappearance.

MARI LIFTED the DeWalt to examine the chip of wood. Leave it to Benuel to discover such a tiny sliver. He constantly amazed her.

"Smell it," he urged.

She did and picked up a faint trace of evergreen. "That's why you were asking about pine trees." How could Benuel tell the difference between pine, spruce, or hemlock? "You're sure it's pine?" She didn't need to hear his answer to know he was certain.

"*Jah*, it is. No doubt about that." He reached over and took the splinter. After sniffing it one more time, he pocketed it again. "Susanna tied Peach's reins to a pine. That's the only clue we have to where she was last."

"But these are the only woods with pines for miles around. Rose said Susanna turned toward home."

"So, either she turned around and drove in the same direction as Rose, or she returned to the school."

"Maybe she forgot something and came back to get it? Or dropped something and was looking for it?"

"But the pony cart tracks only went downhill."

"*Ach*, Benuel. Then she must have gone after Rose. We need to look for her in that direction."

He shook his head. "Maybe not. We should be watching this lane for her tracks coming back."

Mari threw lantern light on the road beside them. Once again, her husband's caution about not walking over the tracks had been the right choice. As they descended, a shadowy area by the trees looked as if it might have been trampled.

"Just let me look over there." She lifted her arm to shine the DeWalt onto the spot, but an engine roared toward them.

Mari jumped to the side, dragging Benuel with her into a small stand of oaks, as a car thundered around the curve. The lantern flew from her hand, crashed into the low tangle of bushes nearby, and went out.

# CHAPTER 7

Fear choked off Susanna's scream. Only one thought flashed through her whirling mind. The hand that held her definitely wasn't a bear. It was human.

A hairy human arm trapped her. She gulped in a breath to scream.

As if sensing her intention, the hand covering her mouth shifted, crushing her nose and her mouth.

She couldn't draw in air. Frantically, she squirmed. She had to get away.

Clutching Snowball tightly to her, Susanna wriggled and jerked, desperate to escape. The arm slammed her back against a rock-hard chest.

Her captor pressed a cold circle of metal to her temple. "Shut up or I'll shoot you and that cat," he growled.

Susanna's heart stopped. Frigid waves of fear sloshed through her body, freezing her muscles, immobilizing her.

When the man shifted, his fingers slipped off her nose. She sucked in air, but her frozen lungs refused to expand. Her chest burned from lack of oxygen. The tiny, shallow breaths she pulled in left her dizzy and lightheaded.

*Please, God, help me.*

The man's hand loosened over mouth. "You make a sound and you're dead."

Susanna choked back a cry.

He clapped the hand back hard. His fingers bit into her cheeks. Tears spurted from her eyes.

A still, small voice inside whispered, *Fear thou not; for I am with thee.*

This time, he lowered the gun hand and held out a dirty rag. He stuffed it into her mouth, twisting it tight. She gagged. He clipped her on the side of the head with the gun.

"Stop it," he ordered.

She had no control over her body. It spasmed into choking. The filthy cloth muffled the strangling noises coming from her throat. Her lungs gasped for air. She drew in shaky breaths, praying she wouldn't pass out.

With one hand gripping her shoulder, he kneed her in the back. "Move it."

Where was he taking her? He pushed her deeper into the woods. The stench got stronger. She wanted to resist, but his fingers dug into her skin, shoving her forward. When she slowed or stumbled over roots, his knee whacked her in the back.

The cold metal of the gun barrel brushed against her skin. He didn't need to keep the gun there. She couldn't cry out. He wanted to frighten her. She wouldn't let him.

Frantically, she searched her memory for every Bible verse about courage she could remember. She recited them one by one:

*Be strong and of a good courage, fear not, nor be afraid of them. . .*

*Yea, though I walk through the valley of the shadow of death, I will fear no evil: for thou art with me. . .*

*For the Lord is on my side; I will not fear. . .*

Repeating God's words over and over strengthened her

and made her braver. Although she was still scared, peace descended over her. The Lord was with her.

*Please help me to be brave, Lord,* she begged.

The trees ahead thinned out into a clearing. The stench choked Susanna. Her eyes burned from the fumes and unshed tears. A chain-link fence filled with snarling pit bulls blocked them from approaching a high, wooden fence beyond it.

Susanna stiffened as the dogs slobbered and snapped, exposing sharp teeth. A few made strangled sounds as if they couldn't bark. Others growled low in their throats, but didn't bark.

The man stopped by the metal fence, dragging Susanna to a stop. "Toss that kitten to the dogs. They'll rip it apart." His cruel laugh sent shivers through her. "We keep 'em hungry so's they attack intruders."

Had she rescued this little fluffball from an eagle only to see it torn to pieces by savage dogs? She planted her feet and refused to move. No way would she allow this tiny baby get hurt. He'd have to toss her to those dogs first.

"Go on." His knee slammed into her back again, propelling her forward.

"What we got here?" A gravelly voice to their left startled Susanna and halted the cruel man tormenting her.

She whipped her head in that direction. A skinny man with stringy, shoulder-length hair and red sores dotting his face smirked at her.

"An Amish girl?" His snarky smile revealed rotting, blackened teeth. "Well, well, Duke'll be pleased to see her. He'll happily take her off our hands."

He squatted. "C'mere, girlie."

Susanna shrank back, but the man holding her shoved her in that direction.

"Move it," he commanded.

*God, help me!* Susanna sent up a desperate plea.

"What's yer name, girlie?"

His teeth reminded her of her *Englisch* neighbors' jack-o'-lanterns after the candles had burned down, leaving behind jagged blackened stubs. She shivered.

He laughed. "You scared of me?"

Susanna froze. Then another verse came to mind: *fear not them which kill the body, but are not able to kill the soul.* Whatever this man did to her, he couldn't touch her soul. That belonged to God. She straightened, drawing herself to her full height.

"That's right. Only one you gots to be afraid of is. . . him." He pointed to the man who'd dragged her here.

Susanna peeped at her kidnapper from the corner of her eye. Tall and broad-shouldered, he towered over them. With his bushy, black beard and huge hairy arms, he resembled a bear as he lumbered toward them. She gulped.

"Enough, Junior. Get back to work."

*Work? What work did they do out here in the middle of the woods?*

Junior scrambled to his feet. "Yessir, boss." He eyed the kitten in Susanna's arms. "You gonna let her keep that there animal?"

The boss flicked his head toward the open wooden gate. "We'll feed it to the dogs soon enough."

*No, you won't.* Susanna had no idea how she'd prevent them, but she'd never let that happen. Maybe she should let the kitten go. But she didn't want to leave it to owls and foxes. She cradled Snowball close.

"If'n you say so." Jagged-teeth Junior nudged Susanna ahead of him toward the high wooden gate that stood ajar a few feet away.

"How many times have I told you never to leave the gate open?" The boss man thundered.

"Sorry, boss. I jest wanted ta see—"

A low, guttural growl cut him off. "Idiot. You don't have the brains God gave a worm."

He believed in God. Susanna stopped so suddenly Junior plowed into her, almost knocking her off her feet. She turned to stare at the boss.

His shaggy black brows crawled together like a hairy caterpillar. He grabbed Junior by the collar of his T-shirt and give him a swift kick. The boss's booted foot hit Junior squarely in the backside, sending him tumbling. With his face contorted in rage, the boss didn't look much like a God-fearing man. The string of curses that issued from his mouth didn't sound godly either.

Junior scrabbled around in the dirt, struggling to get to his feet. He glared balefully at his boss. "T'weren't no call ta do that. Ain't nobody around these parts to see in."

"You don't know that. Anybody could be spying."

*Spying?* What were these men doing?

Inside the gate, a rickety shack filled most of the space. Most windows had been blacked out, but several held industrial-sized fans blowing fumes. Susanna's nostrils stung, and her stomach churned. The overwhelming stink made her nauseous.

Junior shoved her along to the front door, but he halted before he opened it. "What we gonna do with her? We don't want her seein' in here."

"Lock her in one of the sheds for now."

Junior grabbed Susanna's arm and dragged her to the row of sheds along the back fence. They passed burned-out pits. Dead spots dotted the scraggly, dried-out grass. Mounds of used soda bottles, drain opener, paint thinner, and chemical containers littered the back corner of the yard along with rubber gloves and masks. Empty boxes of cold medicine had been thrown on top of the trash heap. Nobody could have that many colds. What were these men doing? And what was causing that awful smell?

Junior let go of her arm and dug in his pocket for a key ring.

Susanna glanced around desperately for an escape. Barbed wire topped the ten-foot-high board fence. All the gaps in the wood had been sealed. The boss had closed and latched the gate from the inside. Five different bars and locks secured it. She could make it to the gate, but she could only reach three of them.

As if he'd sensed she planned to flee, Junior snarled as he shuffled through his keys. "If'n you move, I'll shoot you.

She stilled, but she continued to search her surroundings. The gate was the only way out. Had she missed anything? What would *Daed* notice?

Before she had a chance to check, Junior snapped open the padlock. The door creaked open. He yanked her arm and shoved her inside. The lock snapped shut.

Although it was pitch black inside, Susanna examined her surroundings the way *Daed* might. She touched every surface around her as she waited for her eyes to adjust. They'd jammed her in with cardboard cartons stacked to the ceiling. She barely had room to sit or stand. If she stood on tiptoe, her fingertips brushed the metal roof. She explored the door and all the walls she could reach. The place seemed airtight.

Susanna's heart sank. It seemed impossible she'd ever get out of here.

Panic filled her chest. *Daed* was an excellent detective, but if he searched for her, he'd never find this place. He'd never imagine she go this far into the trees. And even if he did, he'd never think about looking for her here. Besides, he couldn't get past those dogs. Or the guns. If he managed that and got past that gate with its five locks, would he think to check in a locked metal shed for her? Even if he freed her, they'd have no way out.

# CHAPTER 8

*B*efore Mari and Benuel could recover, more buggies raced up the lane, followed by a police cruiser and several cars, obliterating any tracks.

Benuel sighed. "I guess we won't be able to see if Susanna stopped here."

"*Neh*, the ground will be trampled with hooves, buggy wheels, and tire tracks."

"We'd better get up to the schoolhouse and talk to everyone."

"I need to find the light. I hope it didn't break." Mari released Benuel's arm and tromped through the bushes. She soon stopped in frustration. Clouds hid most of the stars in the moonless light, leaving the ground in deep shadow. "I have no idea where it landed."

"About three feet in front of you and a foot or two to your left," Benuel told her. "It crashed through some low brush."

Mari followed his directions and found the DeWalt. She laughed. "I should have let you go after it. You would have found it faster than I did."

"Not on that rough ground."

"Still, your hearing is amazing. I only heard the pounding of hooves." She flicked the switch, and the light turned on. "*Gut*, it still works."

Benuel smiled as she returned and took his arm. "Lead on, my lovely wife. We now have reinforcements to help us search for Susanna."

Although his tone came across as cheery and upbeat, Mari detected a note of fear underlying his words. She snuggled closer to him, trying not to let her own anxiety overwhelm her.

By the time Mari and Benuel made it up the hill, Teacher Rose had unlocked the schoolhouse, and several women had set out urns of coffee and platters of snacks. The police chief and two officers stood in front of a huge map of the area taped to the wall. The chief called for order and beckoned for Mari and Benuel to join him.

Mari tilted her head up to whisper to Benuel. "They want us up front."

He gave her a wan smile. "I could tell."

She didn't bother to ask how he knew. Benuel had his ways.

After they moved to the front of the room, Chief Richardson directed his gaze at Benuel. "Tell us what you know about Susanna's disappearance."

Benuel swallowed hard, and Mari pressed closer to him.

"Only that she didn't come home after school," Benuel said. "Her pony, Peach, raced up the driveway almost two hours after school ended, dragging the pony cart. The cart felt battered. By the road, I think. Not from an accident."

"I see." The chief pursed his lips. "She's not usually so late?"

Mari answered quickly. "*Neh.*"

Teacher Rose spoke up. "Susanna usually hurries home.

46

Today, she dawdled after school. I had to tell her to hitch up her pony, and I waited until she started down the driveway before following her."

"Did she seem to be waiting for someone?" The chief studied Rose as she thought.

Rose's brows pinched together. "*Neh*, I don't think so. She seemed more like—" Rose stopped as if uncertain. "Almost reluctant to leave. Like she had to do something she'd rather not."

Mari's stomach twisted. Had Susanna not wanted to come home because of her?

"Oh, and this was unusual too. This morning when I arrived at the schoolhouse, Susanna was already here, sitting on the swings, looking glum."

Benuel squirmed beside Mari. Did he feel as guilty as she did?

Her husband cleared his throat. "Before school today, Susanna broke a china bird—one of the last presents her *mamm* had given her before she died. She was upset over that. She took off right after breakfast."

Mari pressed closer to Benuel. "Maybe we should tell them. . ." she whispered.

The police chief caught her eye. "Anything else we should know?"

Mari lowered her eyes. "Susanna hasn't adjusted well to our marriage. She seems to resent me."

"Is it possible she'd run away?" His eyes bored into her.

"I-I don't think so."

"But you don't know for sure?"

Shame filled Mari. Had Susanna run away because of her?

Before she could answer, Benuel's voice rang out. "My *dochder* would never run away." And as if sensing Mari's

47

inner thoughts, he inclined his head to whisper. "This is not your fault."

"Anything else you can tell us? Has she been acting differently lately? More secretive? Doing things that are out of character? Does she have access to any electronics?"

Mari gasped. "Of course not." What was he implying?

BENUEL'S STOMACH clenched into a tight knot. Did he think Susanna met someone? Some *Englischers* in his shop discussed the dangers of the internet and that friends had discovered their preteen children texting with grown men. Benuel had been glad Susanna didn't have a phone. And his daughter's busy schedule kept her from that kind of trouble.

Benuel could sense the police chief's gaze raking him and Mari, and he fidgeted. "Mari's right," he said firmly. "Susanna didn't use the internet."

"It's not uncommon for kids to use their friends' devices," the chief said. "Does she play with any of your neighbors?"

Benuel shifted. "Not often. She usually comes straight home from school to help at the store. And she works there most of the day on Saturday." He wracked his brains. Susanna wouldn't have had any time to visit their *Englisch* neighbors, would she?

Beside him, Mari nodded. He felt her movement and was grateful for her support.

"So, you don't think she could have made plans to meet anyone?"

"Of course not," Benuel burst out.

Talking about their neighbors reminded Benuel of Burkey. They hadn't heard from him. Susanna must not have made it back home. And he would have called if he'd located her at an area hospital. Why were they wasting all this time talking instead of searching?

He fidgeted and tried to keep the desperation from his voice. "Can we start looking for Susanna?"

"We have an Amber Alert out for her. And after what happened a few years ago in Lancaster, we have several squad cars cruising the neighborhood."

Benuel froze. Did they think—?

A man had snatched a teen walking home from church. They'd arrested the culprit six months later, but didn't find the body until months after that. Benuel couldn't let his mind go there.

Hidden behind the folds of her skirt, Mari's fingers sought his. He clung to her hand unsure if she needed reassurance or if she was trying to comfort him. He squeezed her hand gently. They both needed comfort.

"Do we know where she was last seen?" The chief pinned Rose with a searching gaze.

"I guess I was the last one to see her?" Rose glanced around the room and was met with nods. "I went down the driveway after her in my buggy. She turned left, and I turned right."

"You think she headed home?"

"I did keep an eye on her in the rearview mirror until she disappeared from sight where the road bends."

"So we know she made it to the bend. Let's start there." A pained look crossed his face. "It would be easier in daylight. We don't want damage any clues."

Benuel sighed. Everyone already had by driving up to the school. Susanna's tracks had been wiped out.

As if she understood what he was thinking, Mari pressed her fingers against his. He returned the pressure, then disengaged his hand. He didn't want people to notice them holding hands.

"Let's get you broken into teams for a preliminary search along the roadway. For now, we'll just do a visual search, looking for any sign of Susanna. She might have fallen out of the cart and be lying near the road. Keep calling out for her in case she's hurt or hidden from view."

Benuel tensed. He and Mari had already done that as they drove to the schoolhouse. Well, Mari had. He'd only waited for her and prayed. But it couldn't hurt to comb the area one more time in case they'd missed her or a clue.

"Just keep to the shoulder and call her name," the chief continued. "Note any signs of the ground being disturbed or any items that might belong to her. Don't touch anything. Just call in and report it. We'll send an officer to check."

Although he longed to search, Benuel intended to stay here. He'd only slow the teams down and could contribute little.

"Anyone who has a cell phone, please stand over here." The chief waved to his right. "Those with lanterns or powerful flashlights on my left. We'll assign at least one cell and two lights to every group of four."

"What if we have both?" someone joked.

The chief laughed. "Go stand by the door. You can lead your group."

In short order, all the *Englischers* and Amish in the room had been sorted into teams.

The chief gestured to the map. A heavy red marker had traced Susanna's usual route home from school. "We'll focus on this area, of course, but I'd like some teams to take alternate routes. Officers Hess and Musselman have broken this down into sections."

Officer Hess moved around the room, handing out assignments and the number to call if they spotted Susanna. Officer Musselman took down names and contact numbers for everyone in each group.

Several older ladies from the *g'may* offered cups of hot coffee and snacks to the crowd. "We'll stay here as long as it takes. Come back whenever you're hungry or need to warm up."

One by one, the groups filed out the door, until only Benuel, Mari, and the chief were left.

He eyed them curiously. "Probably best you stay here, but you didn't want to join the search?"

"I'd just slow everyone down." Inside, Benuel railed at his helplessness, but he did have some skills he could use later. "I'm happy to help if they find any clues."

"Word around the office is you've done some interesting detective work."

Benuel nodded. "And I'll do what I can if. . ." His throat closed. *If what?* He closed his mind off to the worst possibilities.

# CHAPTER 9

*S*usanna sank onto the chilly metal floor of the shed. The kitten in her arms meowed and wiggled. She set it down. Snowball would be safe in here for now.

Tiny claws scritch-scratched across the floor as Snowball explored their prison. The kitty pounced. She must have caught a bug. Were there mice in here?

Susanna hated creepy-crawly things like spiders. Mice were even worse. At the thought of a mouse creeping over her in the dark, she shivered, bent her legs close to her body, and wrapped her skirt and arms protectively around them.

What was she going to do? She had to find her own way out. But how?

She had no way to pry open the door. If she did have tools, would she be strong enough?

*Lord, please show me what to do. And help me keep Snowball safe.*

Minutes ticked into hours. At least it seemed like hours. The metal behind her back grew colder and colder. Her teeth chattered. Fall nights sometimes dipped into frosty weather.

Snowball's fur should keep her warm, but what about me? Will I freeze in here?

Outside the shed, boots clumped through fallen leaves. Her stomach clenched. Were they coming for her? What did they plan to do to her?

The door rattled. Someone lifted the lock. Metal scratched against metal. The lock. They were unlocking it.

She hunched into a tighter ball as the door creaked open. A bright light shone into her eyes.

"Don't hurt me," she whimpered.

"Ain't gonna do nothing to ya long as you do what I say. All I need is that there vest you is wearing."

*Her safety vest?* "Why?"

He sighed. "I gotta go drop it somewheres. Somewheres far from here. Out toward them farms." He waved toward the woods Susanna had plodded through earlier.

This time she didn't need to ask why. They intended to throw searchers off track. Send them in the wrong direction.

Her *g'may* would be looking for her by now. She couldn't let these men misdirect them. Although she doubted they'd come this way. Nobody would expect her to come into the woods. They'd follow her route home from school. Still, she didn't want to help them plant false clues.

She lifted her chin. "What if I won't give it to you?"

The light lowered out of her eyes as he shrugged. The small beam of light cast backward around his face revealed a teen with reddish fuzz on his upper lip and a few scraggly hairs on his chin. His eyes held a flat, bored look, and he had small sores on his face. Did they have a skin disease that was catching?

He flicked the flashlight. "I ain't gonna wait all night. Either ya give it to me, or I take it off."

Susanna cowered. She didn't want him to touch her. What if she got that rash?

Despite the toughness of his words, this boy seemed jittery. Scared even. *Daed* always watched people's movements, listened to hidden sounds under their words. This teen seemed softer than the other two. Maybe he'd help her.

"What's your name?" she asked.

Startled, he took a step back. "None a your business."

"I'm Susanna."

"Yeah, well, Susanna, if ya don't gimme that vest, I'm gonna take it off ya." He sounded reluctant to do that.

*Gut.* Hope flickered in Susanna's chest. Maybe, just maybe. . .

"You don't really want to do that, do you?"

He fidgeted. "Don't matter none what I want. Boss man say do it, I do it."

"But won't you get in trouble with the police? Do you want to go to jail?"

"Shut up. You ain't scaring me none."

But she'd rattled him.

"Please, don't do this. Let me go. My *daed* and *mamm* will be worried about me being so late."

For the first time since *Daed* married Mari, Susanna had called her stepmother *Mamm*. Right now, she'd run into Mari's arms if only she could see her. She'd run into anyone's arms. Anyone except these strangers.

"Just gimme that vest." His gruff tone didn't hide his uncertainty.

Tears sprang to Susanna's eyes at the thought of hugging Mari.

*God, I promise to be nicer to her if you'll help me get out of here.*

She tried to appeal to his softer side. "Wouldn't your parents miss you if someone kidnapped you?"

His bark of laughter startled her. "Ain't got no dad. Never did. And my maw's too drunk to look fer me."

"I'm sorry." Susanna's heart went out to him. She understood what it was like to be missing a parent. And to have a mother who wouldn't even search for him?

A white flash darted past his boots. "What the—?"

Susanna scooped her up. "It's Snowball. My kitty."

Neo groaned. "Boss ain't gonna like it." He shone the light over the small, furry body.

A voice screamed from a distance. "Neo? What's taking so long?"

Susanna covered her ears at the curses that followed.

The teen bent over her. "Gimme that."

Susanna backed away from his grabby hands. "I'll take it off." As she did, she asked, "Is Neo your name?"

He snatched the vest from her hands. "What's it to ya?"

"I want to know what to call you."

"Why?"

"It's friendlier to call people by their names."

"Friendlier?" He snorted. "Where yer going, kid, you won't be wanting to know no names. Less'n yer planning to report 'em."

Shivers ran through her. "Where am I going?"

Neo—if that was his name—faltered. Dropped his gaze and looked uncomfortable.

"Duke keeps kids fer. . ." He waved his hand. "You know. . ."

Susanna shook her head. *Neh*, she didn't know. But the expression on his face scared her.

"Neo, please help me. Let me go. Open the gate. I won't tell the police about anything."

For a moment, he studied her, his eyes filled with compassion. Then he straightened up, and his eyes hardened. He whirled on his heels. "I ain't taking no chances."

"Could you get me some water and food? I'm hungry

and thirsty." Would appealing for his help in other ways soften him? Would he care?

"Nothing I can do. I gots to take care of this." He waved the vest in the air.

"Please?" she begged.

Neo didn't answer. He just stormed out of the shed, slammed the door, and snapped the padlock into place with a loud click. A click of finality.

*Please, Lord, touch his heart. Send help.*

In a few seconds, a motorcycle rumbled past the shed.

"Junior," Neo shouted above the roar.

He idled by the gate. A short while later, the engine revved, zoomed off to her right, circled behind the fence and whined off up the hill.

They must have a road or path coming in from the mountaintop or the valley on the other side. She'd lived here all her life, but had never seen a road anywhere along the valley or ridge. As far as she—or anyone around here— knew, the woods covered that whole area. Nobody would know that road or this place existed.

Susanna's spirits spiraled into despair. Would God save her from these men? Or did He have another plan?

# CHAPTER 10

$\mathcal{B}$enuel's mind raced. They were more than an hour away from Lancaster, and they'd jailed the man who'd killed that Amish girl. Plus, they were almost an hour from the city of Harrisburg and far from other large cities with their assaults, kidnappings, and murders. The rural areas here had a low crime rate, especially for violent crime. He had to stop imagining worst-case scenarios.

*Please, Lord, protect Susanna wherever she is.*

As if she'd read his mind, Mari sidled nearer. "Let's pray together."

Benuel smiled down at his sweetheart. "I'd like that." He quoted one of his favorite verses: *"For where two or three are gathered together in my name, there am I in the midst of them."*

Chief Richardson shifted uneasily as they bent their heads together. "Excuse me. I need to make a phone call."

He pulled his cell from his pocket and stepped out of the building. After lighting a cigarette, he paced up and down past the schoolhouse windows.

When Benuel and Mari finished praying for Susanna's

protection and lifted their heads, tears sparkled in Mari's eyes. "Whatever happens, God is with her."

Outside the door, Chief Richardson flicked away his cigarette butt. He probably thought his conversation was private, but Benuel picked up most of it.

"Yep, got them all searching along the roads." He sighed. "You don't want to discourage volunteers, but I hope they don't disturb any clues."

Benuel seethed. The chief sounded as if he'd been placating the searchers rather than relying on their help.

"If they don't find anything, I'll get SAR out here in the morning. Supposedly, the girl headed toward home, but if she didn't. . ."

The chief left his words hanging, making it sound as if he thought Susanna had run off.

*SAR?* The chief didn't plan to call out Search and Rescue now? Benuel leaned close to Mari's ear. "We have to find Susanna. It's too cold for here to be out there all night. They're not even going to do an official search until tomorrow."

"How do you know?"

"I heard the chief say so."

"He's outside." Then she poked him gently with her elbow. "You and that hearing of yours. So, you've been eavesdropping?"

Benuel tipped his head in acknowledgment. "Guilty as charged."

When the chief returned, Benuel said to Mari in a voice loud enough to be overheard, "Let's get a breath of fresh air."

They retrieved their coats from the cloakroom, picked up the DeWalt, and slipped outside. Although he'd taken Mari's arm for guidance, Benuel nudged her to the opposite side of the playground.

"I don't think they can hear us here," he whispered. "Do you think I should tell the police about the torn reins?" For some reason, he'd hesitated over sharing that with the police. Would it even matter if they didn't plan to do a real search until tomorrow?

MARI TURNED off the lantern when they'd stopped walking. She wanted to save the battery.

Benuel's question jogged her memory. "I forgot all about the reins with everything else going on. That reminds me. We didn't get to look at that spot I saw in the trees."

"Do you remember where it was?"

"Not exactly, but I did lose the lantern in the bushes. I'm sure we can find where I crushed bushes to find it."

"Perfect. This may not lead to Susanna, but at least I'll feel like I'm doing something."

Mari switched the light back on and led the way to the edge of the driveway they'd used to reach the schoolhouse. "The lane curves near that spot."

"That should make it easier to find."

"*Jah.*" Mari shivered and pulled her cloak more tightly around her. "The temperature is dropping." She hated to think about Susanna being out in the cold.

Mari held the light high overhead to watch for obstacles in front of Benuel and picked up her pace. When they neared the bend, she slowed.

Benuel choked and waved a hand in front of his nose. "That horrid smell is getting worse. We must be close to that place."

"We are." She sniffed the air as they walked, but couldn't detect any odor. "It's right around here somewhere." She stopped suddenly. "This is it." She'd flattened the undergrowth as she'd tramped through it to get the DeWalt.

Beside her, Benuel tensed. "And you saw something across the lane?"

"*Jah*, let's cross over." Lifting the lantern, she shone it across the dirt path. "There's a small clearing over there on the other side." The ground had definitely been disturbed. As they got closer, Mari sucked in a breath.

"What is it?"

"Benuel," Mari's voice quavered with excitement. "Hoof prints. And possible pony cart tracks."

His face brightened. "Lead me to them. Without stepping on them, that is."

She guided him close to the indentations. "Squat here." When he hunkered down, she took his hand and placed it in one of the tracks.

"*Ach*, Mari," he breathed as he felt along the ground, "this must be where Peach tore free. All the hoof prints are small, so they belong to a pony. And look how they change in depth." He fingered the ground. "The shallow ones show where he was tied up."

After Benuel's explanation, Mari could see the differences.

"And these deeper ones show Peach was agitated. She stomped around, getting more restless." He moved his hand along to the final indentations. "Then she dug in. See how deep these are?"

As usual, he was right. The grooves in the ground revealed Peach's desperation to break free. Mari stared at her husband in awe.

~

BENUEL WAS impatient to solve this, praying it would help him discover what Susanna had been doing. "If I follow the arc of the last deep hoof prints, I might figure out where Peach was tied."

He crept along on hands and knees, touching the tracks and feeling in front of him. Several times, sharp rocks pierced his knees through his broadfall trousers. Mari would have quite a bit of mending after this.

When he reached the beginning marks, he stood. "From here, I'll estimate the length of the reins. Will you help me, Mari?" The last thing he needed was to trip and fall.

In an instant, Mari reached his side and slipped his hand into the crook of her arm. His heart overflowed with love at her gentle touch and her support. She steered him around problem areas as he charged forward.

"The reins were about this long." He stopped and sniffed the air. That awful stench burned his nostrils, but if he wanted to find the right tree, he had to keep going. Under the sting of the ammonia, the gentle scent of pine teased his senses.

"We need to check the pine trees closest to us." He swept his arm around in a circle.

From her movements, Mari's head followed the direction of his hand. "We have a lot of pine trees in front of us."

"But Susanna would have used one closest to the road and to the clearing, don't you think?"

"As usual, you're right." She removed his hand from her arm. "Stay here a second. I'll check those."

"It won't be one with low-hanging branches. The trunk needs to be bare at least as high as Susanna would reach."

"That's true."

Benuel carefully noted her footfalls as she moved straight ahead, then stepped left and right. Once again, he wished he could be the one studying the trees, leading the search for his *dochder*.

*Why, Lord, why?*

It was so hard to depend on others, even his beloved Mari. And even harder to wait for answers about Susanna's whereabouts.

# CHAPTER 11

*B*ehind Susanna's back, the metal shed wall chilled her. She shivered and scooted forward as the temperature dropped, huddling into a small ball. Her stomach growled. The stinky fumes made her nauseous, and she buried her nose in her skirt, which she'd stretched over her knees and tucked around her ankles. She played with the kitten for a little while before wrapping her arms around her legs again, trying to stay warm.

*Lord, I'm hungry, cold, and scared. Please, please, help me. And I need food for Snowball.*

The kitten had pounced on several bugs, so maybe she'd eaten a little. Susanna dreamed of home. She imagined *Daed* hugging her the way he'd done this morning as she cried over the china bird. She'd pushed out of his arms because she'd been angry at him. When she'd walked down the steps, he'd been embracing Mari. *If only I could feel his arms around me now.*

*If only I could be home in my warm bed. If only I could wrap my arms around Peach's neck and—*

She shot up straight. *Peach!* What about her pony? Peach must be hungry and cold. *If I hadn't been so foolish, my pony would be warm inside her stall, eating hay.*

Were *Daed* and Mari looking for her? Would they find Peach?

Susanna prayed for Peach's safety, recited Bible verses, and prayed some more. She bargained with God, promising to make peace with Mari if He sent someone to rescue her.

A motorcycle buzzed past the shed. Neo must be back. Where had he left her safety vest? Would *Daed* be looking for her in the wrong place? Would they call in the police? Everyone would head in the wrong direction. They'd never find her here.

Although the fans from the house made a racket, *Daed* had taught her to listen for softer sounds underneath. Faint footsteps reached her ears. Something crinkled right outside the shed. The door rattled.

Susanna's pulse galloped. Was it Neo? What did he want?

More crinkling and rattling accompanied the scritch of metal in the lock. Then the door swung open. Light dazzled her eyes. Then it lowered.

A hunchback with a hood over his head stood in the doorway.

Susanna swallowed a scream.

"You okay?" a gruff voice asked.

She recognized that voice. "Neo?"

"Yeah." He stepped inside the shed.

The smell of greasy fried food tantalized her. Her mouth watered, and her stomach grumbled. He'd bought himself a fast-food meal. Had he brought it in here to torture her?

When the light shifted, it framed a blanket draped over Neo's head and shoulders. Folds of blanket formed the lump on his back.

He stepped over to her and held out the bag. "Here." He shuffled his feet, looking embarrassed. "You said you was hungry."

Tears stung Susanna's eyes. "I am." She lowered her knees so she could clutch the semi-warm bag to her chest, thankful for that tiny bit of warmth. And for the food. His kindness sent floods of gratitude through her.

Neo set a milkshake beside her. Then he unwound the blanket from around his neck. "Sorry it's scuzzy. Me and Junior lay on it ta fix engines."

The odors of oil and gas stung Susanna's nose as he settled the rough wool blanket around her. She wanted to thank him, but her throat had tightened from the tears she was fighting.

But he wasn't done. He pulled a small, ragged towel from his neck. He cleared his throat. "Bed for yer cat."

"Oh, Neo." Drops she'd been struggling to hold back trickled down her cheeks.

He looked uncomfortable as he turned away. "I ain't got no cat food."

"I'll share my milkshake." She held out a tiny bite of hamburger. Snowball sniffed the air and scampered over. Susanna picked up the kitten and set it on her lap.

While Neo prowled the small shed, she bit into the cheeseburger. She almost groaned as the tang of sauce, melted cheese, lukewarm lettuce, chewy burger, and soggy bun filled her mouth.

Sauce and tomato juice dribbled down her chin. She set the burger back in its box to wipe every drip onto her finger. She wouldn't waste any of this meal. Had she ever tasted anything this *gut*?

Snowball batted at her hand as she picked up her sandwich. Susanna took out the Styrofoam burger box and set it on the cat's towel. She broke off a few tidbits of meat and set them in one side of the container. Then she poured some milkshake into the other side. Ignoring the meat, Snowball lapped hungrily at the icy liquid.

Meanwhile, Neo's flashlight played over the cardboard cartons, revealing cases of soda, coffee filters, antifreeze, and drain opener. "*Hmm*, you got soda here too. So you got stuff ta drink." He wrestled down the top box and ripped open the lid. "There ya go."

"*Danke*, I mean thank you, Neo. Did you have anything to eat?" She started to break her burger in half.

"Naw. You gonna need all a that food. Duke don't come till day after tomorrow. I can't feed ya more." He looked touched. "I already ate."

"You sure?" Susanna studied him to be sure he was telling the truth. Under his threadbare T-shirt, she suspected his ribs showed. She'd never seen anyone that thin.

He bounced from foot to foot as if nervous under her scrutiny. "Junior he make stuff ta eat most nights. We got crackers and cookies and all."

"*Dank*— Thank you again, Neo. This was so nice of you. I prayed, and you came to help."

"I ain't nobody's answer ta prayer."

Susanna smiled. "*God works in mysterious ways.*"

"Yeah, right." Neo rolled his eyes. "I gotta go." He rushed for the door but turned back to her. "Hide them wrappers when you done. Don't want Boss ta know."

He slipped out of the shed, eased the door shut, and clicked the lock gently as if trying to make as little noise as possible. With the loud fans blowing, Susanna didn't know why he bothered being quiet. Nobody could hear anything over that racket.

*Danke, Lord, danke!*

As she finished the last bite of sandwich and drained her

milkshake, Susanna's gratitude spilled over into song. She lifted her voice in the words of *"Das Loblied,"* the song of thanksgiving they sang every Sunday.

Yet, one nagging fear marred her joy. Would she ever join her church in singing praises again?

# CHAPTER 12

*M*ari headed in the direction Benuel had pointed, examining each evergreen tree, searching for exposed lower trunks. Most had full branches sweeping the ground or short, stubby trunks. None matched Benuel's description.

She wandered a little farther off the road. A few saplings stood close to the clearing. Raising her light, she moved closer. "Here, Benuel," she called. She raced over to him.

He grabbed her arm, and she guided him to the tree. She stepped aside as he ran his hands up and down over the scraped-off bark.

"See how deep some of these grooves are?" he remarked. "Peach really struggled, didn't she?"

"*Jah*, she did." Mari didn't want to discourage him, but suppose it hadn't been Susanna but some other child who'd stopped here?

Benuel dropped to the ground and felt around the base of the tree. "*Ah-ha!* Here they are." He held up the broken ends of the reins.

Mari had been so busy focusing on the height of tree

trunks, she hadn't shone her light on the ground. She should have thought of looking for the reins.

"Now we know Susanna was here."

The relief in his voice made Mari long to hug him. He hadn't shown his nervousness, but now she could tell how worried he'd been.

"I'm going to check for footprints."

He'd entered full detective mode. She admired his painstaking examination of each area of the ground. Not even a tiny twig escaped his notice.

He held up one that had snapped. "Someone stepped on this. See the way it's broken?" He'd kept his other hand at the spot. "*Jah*, her heel must have crunched down on it. But here's the front of her sneaker."

Mari's heartrate sped up. She never would have seen that faint impression. But it was definitely the front of a footprint. "I wonder why she stopped here."

"Can you see more prints?" Benuel asked eagerly.

Sweeping the light across the clearing, Mari searched for more depressions in the ground. "A few more." She frowned. "But after the tree line, the ground is covered with leaves and needles."

"Is there a path?"

"Not really. The trees grow close together."

"Hmm… maybe she just stopped here and walked somewhere. I wonder if Peach got loose, and Susanna ran after the departing pony cart."

"She might have."

"I'll see if I can trace Peach's hooves down the hill, and check for Susanna's footprints. If they stayed close to the woods at first, we might find their tracks."

"Good idea." Mari wanted to stay with Benuel, but he'd be fine as long as he crawled along the ground. He felt in front of him before he moved forward. "Maybe I

69

should stay here and look for more footprints in the clearing."

$\sim$

BENUEL TRIED NOT to let his disappointment show. He'd rather have Mari with him, but her idea made sense. "We'll cover more ground that way."

"Let's keep calling for her."

"*Jah*, we should have been doing that all along." Benuel headed downhill following the tracks and yelling Susanna's name.

Mari's voice echoed through the trees. He liked being able to tell where she was all the time. The cart tracks and Peach's prints were easy to find in the damp dirt. He made it almost halfway down the hill without locating any sneaker prints. Maybe Susanna hadn't run after the pony. Still, he'd keep going.

The searchers had been assigned places starting at the bend in the road. He'd holler Susanna's name all the way to that spot.

A muscle car screeched around the corner and into the lane, the bass thumping so loudly it rocked the car and assaulted his eardrums. Benuel clapped his hands over his ears, hoping to block some of the clamor.

The driver slammed on the brakes and fishtailed, spraying gravel that pelted Benuel.

"Are you all right?" the teen screamed over the strident discord.

Benuel could barely make out the words, but he didn't want to remove his hands from his ears. The next thing he knew, three teens—he could tell from their young and firm arm muscles—lifted Benuel to his feet.

"Are you hurt?" one boy shouted close to Benuel's ear.

"Maybe he's drunk," another teen suggested.

"I don't smell any alcohol."

"The music," Benuel said, unable to function with that driving drumbeat drilling into his skull and sending shockwaves through his jaw.

"Hey, Axel, turn that down some. This guy can't hear."

The music lowered a few decibels.

"That better?"

"A little," Benuel conceded.

"Lower, Axel," someone else shouted.

The music still rattled Benuel's bones, but he endured it as best he could and tried to participate in the loud conversation.

"What happened, man?" the teen supporting his elbow asked. "You fall down?"

Benuel shook his head and wished he hadn't. The pounding made him dizzy. "I was feeling for tracks." Tracks that would now be erased with all the scuffling feet around him.

"In the dark? Why didn't you just use a flashlight?"

"Are the Amish allowed to use flashlights?" his friend asked.

"We are," Benuel responded, "but I'm blind."

"Whoa. But shouldn't you wear one of those florescent things that shine in the dark?"

"Maybe the Amish can't use those," his friend suggested.

"Sure they can. I see the kids with them all the time when they're walking home from school."

The teen, who still held Benuel's arm, asked solicitously, "You need help getting somewhere? We got some other friends coming, and I don't want them to hit you like we almost did."

"I wasn't expecting anyone to be coming up this road at night."

The boy shuffled his feet a little. "Yeah, well, we sometimes come up here for, um— Well, we get together."

"And listen to music and stuff."

Benuel had a feeling he could guess what stuff. "Tonight's not a good night for that. There are people in the schoolhouse."

"Doing what? Nobody's ever up here."

"Looking for my missing daughter."

"Whoa. We better call this off."

"Ya think?" One of the boys punched buttons on his phone. "Tell everyone not to come to the schoolhouse. Some Amish chick's gone missing. We'll have to meet at the park."

"Maybe we should stay here and help." The leader seemed uncertain. "You need help, man?" he asked Benuel. "We can get people together to look for your girl. How old is she?"

"Twelve." Benuel tried to decide if the teens with their pulsating music would be a help or hindrance. "They have search parties assigned to different areas."

"You were assigned here? Want us to look for you?"

Now that Benuel thought about it, these boys could check the tracks easier and faster. "Let me show you the trail I was following." He pointed to a place behind him. "Do you see the hoof prints? And the lines of the cart wheels."

"Gotta turn on our phone lights." The leader stepped away from Benuel's side. "Yeah," he said excitedly. "I see them."

"Can you tell where they go?"

"Oh, looks like we messed them up here." He stepped past Benuel. "They start again over there." He moved farther downhill. After a short while, he returned. "They veer off into the center of the road a short distance from here. Then there's too many other tracks to see where they go."

Benuel's shoulders slumped. "That's what I was afraid of." This had been a dead end. "Guess I'd better go back to my wife. She was looking farther up the hill."

"I can help you up there if you want."

"Thank you, um. . . I don't even know your name."

"Coltrane, sir."

"Benuel." He extended his hand, and the teen shook it.

"How do we do this?" Coltrane sounded nervous.

"If you crook your arm, I'll hold on to it. You just lead the way and steer me around anything that'll trip me up."

They traversed the hill. As that ammonia stench increased, Benuel waved toward the side of the road. "Is there a clearing over there?"

"I see one up ahead."

"That's where my wife is."

"You sure? I don't see anyone, but I'll check."

Now that they were far away from the car, the ringing in Benuel's ears had stopped. But the music vibrated through the trees and into the soles of his feet. He didn't hear Mari calling for Susanna. Had she gotten cold and gone into the schoolhouse? Why hadn't she let him know? Maybe she had, and he hadn't heard her over the din.

Coltrane lifted his arm and swept his phone over the area. "Benuel, this clearing's empty."

"Mari must have gone up to the building. It's pretty cold out."

"I'll take you up there." Coltrane guided Benuel to the schoolhouse door and opened it for him.

"Thank you so much." Benuel shook Coltrane's hand. "Couldn't have done it without you."

"If you need us, I'm Coltrane Zimmerman. Just give us a call. We'll come out to help."

"I appreciate it." Benuel stepped over the threshold and

waited for Mari to take his arm as the door swung shut. But she didn't hurry over.

"Where's your wife?" Chief Richardson asked.

"She's not here?

"Haven't seen her since the two of you stepped outside." A note of suspicion laced the chief's voice. "What were you two doing? Plotting where to hide the body?"

# CHAPTER 13

*A*s soon as Benuel started off, Mari shouted for Susanna and moved back to the last footprint they'd found. The ground had been disturbed right after that. It almost looked like someone had tussled here. She tilted her light to get a better view.

The beam shone through a gap in the trees. Was that another footprint? Mari stepped closer. It might be. She squeezed through the trees. *Jah*, it was.

Excited, she swung the lantern from side to side looking for the next print. *Ach!* There it was. But the prints grew longer as if Susanna had been shuffling along. Or maybe running and kicking up the leaves. Benuel would know. Mari wished he were here.

Had something or someone been chasing Susanna?

Mari searched for other footprints or pawprints. She found none.

"Susanna? Susanna?"

On the hill below, a roaring engine drowned out Benuel's cries for Susanna. Mari hoped the car wouldn't race up here. The blaring music overpowered all the other sounds.

The car didn't seem to be moving. It hadn't run into Benuel, had it? Mari shivered at the thought.

*Please keep Benuel safe, Lord.*

Maybe the car hadn't turned into the lane. Or the driver had stopped to talk to Benuel. Mari forced herself to keep going. Benuel would have heard the car long before it approached, and he'd have gotten out of the way. He had such good instincts.

She relaxed a little, but she wished the driver would turn down the music so she could hear her husband. The beat shaking the car pulsed through the earth under her feet. That drew her attention back to the footprints.

"Susanna? Susanna?"

Overhead, an owl hooted, startling Mari. She jumped, messing up some of the footprints.

She froze as rustling came from the bushes nearby. A small animal frightened by the owl? Or by the pounding music?

She longed for Benuel's presence. She wanted to clutch his hand, to feel his arm around her shoulders, drawing her close. His rock steady peacefulness in a crisis always calmed her jangled nerves.

Wind creaked the branches overhead. Or was that the owl?

The *whoo* came again.

Something skittered near her feet. Mari jumped back, her heart hammering. She pressed a hand to her chest and struggled to draw in air. Every noise around her sounded ominous.

Had these sounds frightened Susanna? Maybe that's why she'd run.

Mari clutched the lantern tighter, lifted it higher, and cast its beam all around her. Light might scare away beasts.

When her pulse slowed a little, Mari squeaked out Susanna's name. She cleared her throat. Tried again.

She gulped in a breath and choked. Then she gasped. *Ach!* The smell Benuel described.

*How horrible! Why does the woods smell like rotten eggs?* She sniffed again. *And—and is that ammonia?*

*Jah*, it did smell like ammonia. Where was it coming from? She'd rather not find out. But she had to find Susanna.

Taking only shallow breaths, Mari followed Susanna's trail. Another patch of scattered leaves extended into the undergrowth. Had Susanna fallen? Or had an animal come along and obscured her footprints?

Mari examined the markings. Probably an animal. Something had crawled around here or rolled in these leaves. Her mouth dried. Had an animal attacked her stepdaughter?

*Please, God,* neh!

If only Benuel were here. He'd understand these clues. Mari had to press on. Her throat too dry to call out, she moved beyond the large tangle of leaves, searching for more footprints.

*There!* A footprint emerged from a scrubby tangle of brush. What had Susanna been doing in those bushes?

Mari soldiered on past the jumbled leaves, hoping and praying the tracks continued. Far on the other side, she discovered another trail.

*Danke*, Lord!

At times, the prints spun in a different direction as if Susanna had turned to look around. Had she heard something? Seen something? In one place, she'd backed into the undergrowth.

The trees narrowed. Mari slid her arm with the DeWalt through the gap between the trunks, then edged herself sideways through the small opening. She breathed easier on the other side. The indentations continued for several more feet.

Mari hurried forward. Then the trail ended. She turned in a circle, frantic to find more prints. But she spotted none.

She'd come to a dead end.

Impossible! Susanna couldn't have just disappeared.

Tamping down her panic, Mari checked the trees. Had Susanna climbed one to get away from an animal?

Mari choked out Susanna's name.

*Please, Lord, help me find her.*

One by one, Mari illuminated the branches above her, trying to examine them the way Benuel would. What would he check for? Listen for?

Nothing stood out to her, so she turned her attention to the vegetation around the last footprints. To her left, twigs and branches lay cracked and strewn across a rough path. The opening appeared the right size for a person.

Or a bear.

Mari's breath caught in her throat. Had Susanna been carried off by a bear?

If so, should Mari follow her? That might be foolish. She needed help.

Loud crashing echoed through the trees. Branches cracked and shattered. Heavy footfalls pounded toward her. Was whatever grabbed Susanna coming for her?

*a*t the vibes coming off Chief Richardson, Benuel stiffened. Surely, the police couldn't possibly believe he'd killed his own daughter. "I love Susanna. I wouldn't do anything to hurt her. Neither would Mari."

"Parents sometimes lose their tempers. Get carried away."

"I'd never—"

"Where's your wife?" Richardson shot the question at Benuel like a bullet aimed at his heart.

"I don't know." Panic filled his chest. "I need to go back out and search for her." He fumbled for the doorknob behind him, but the chief crossed the room in two strides and clamped a meaty hand on Benuel's arm.

"The only place you're going is over here to answer questions." Richardson propelled Benuel to a metal folding chair and plunked him down.

"Don't move while I make some calls."

As he had before, the chief went outside the door.

Benuel concentrated on the conversation.

"Put out an APB on Mari Miller." The chief went on to describe her.

Benuel drank in the details hungrily. He'd never seen his wife's eye or hair color, but he'd explored the texture of her skin and hair. He knew every inch of her body and her moods, her likes and dislikes, her soul. But he didn't even know what color dress she had on today.

That slashed at his heart. Suppose he'd been the only one with her on a day she went missing. He couldn't have described her to people. For that matter, he had no idea what dress Susanna had worn today.

And now he sat here uselessly when Mari could be out there hurt or lost. Where would she have gone? Had she gone farther into the woods? But why?

That strange odor bothered him. Had someone dumped something illegally in the woods? Suppose Mari ran into the people doing it? Would they harm her?

Benuel sat bolt upright. Could that be what happened to Susanna? Her sense of smell was almost as keen as his. Had that stench made her curious, and she'd gone to investigate? Maybe she'd gotten lost in the woods. He tried not to think of a more sinister possibility.

Mari might be following those clues. He prayed she was, but he needed to be with her to keep her safe.

Chief Richardson's voice sank to a whisper. "And get a search warrant for the Benuel Miller property. House, barn, any outbuildings, and the grounds."

*What!?* Benuel tensed.

After barking a few more orders, the chief snapped. "Call me right away if anything turns up."

A few seconds later, the door banged open. Heavy boots thudded across the floor toward Benuel. A chair leg scraped across the floor. The metal creaked as the police chief lowered himself into it.

Benuel burst out, "Why are you searching our house when you should be out looking for Susanna? And Mari?"

"How do you know about that?" His question had an angry edge.

"I heard you."

"Overheard, you mean? How did you get to the door to eavesdrop and get back to your chair so quickly? You just pretending to be blind?"

"I didn't move from this chair. I have good hearing."

"Nobody's hearing's that good."

"Mine is."

The chief called to the women manning the refreshment table. "Could any of you hear my phone conversation when I was outside?"

A chorus of *neh*'s answered him.

"Did this man go over to the door?"

The women's loud *neh*'s carried an undertone of puzzlement.

"He's been right there the whole time," one offered helpfully. "And he didn't ask any of us to guide him."

"Impossible."

Benuel didn't want to waste time on arguing. Now that he had an idea of where Susanna may have gone, he wanted to rush out there to check. His *dochder* might be lost and afraid. Or worse. If she surprised someone in illegal activities, who knows what they'd do.

The woods held other dangers. Bears sometimes attacked people. Animals could be rabid. If Susanna had tripped or hurt herself. . .

*Please, Lord, keep my mind from imagining the worst. And protect Susanna and Mari from wild animals and all other dangers in the woods.*

Richardson rocked the chair as he shifted around to face Benuel. He muttered almost to himself, "When I took this job, they told me you had super powers, but I didn't believe them."

Benuel had mainly worked with the FBI, but the local police had been involved in the cases. Chief Richardson had only come on board after Mari's kidnapping, so the chief hadn't seen what Benuel could do. Still, he didn't want anyone believing he had super powers. "Any abilities I have are God-given."

"Sure, sure." The chief brushed that aside. "Now, why did you and your wife go outside?"

"To search for my daughter."

"Like you could find anything." The chief's words dripped with scorn.

Benuel bristled. People often underestimated him. Just because he couldn't see, they discounted him as worthless. "Mari and I found—"

The chief cut him off. "What happened to your wife? Did you send her off to cover up the crime?" His chair creaked as he leaned nearer. His hot breath fanned Benuel's face. "Or did you do something to her?"

Without waiting for an answer, Richardson rushed on. "Was she threatening to expose the truth?"

Benuel's teeth clenched. He tried to keep his tone calm and firm. "I left Mari at the clearing where. . ." His words trailed off as he tried to recall the last place Mari stood before he set off down the road. She'd been at the pine with Susanna's reins below it.

What had he done with the reins?

He'd shown them to Mari. Had she held onto them? He furrowed his brow, trying desperately to remember each detail.

Richardson broke into Benuel's thoughts. "Trying to come up with an alibi? What'd you do to her?"

"Nothing. I need to get out there and find her and Susanna." *Now!* They could be in danger.

The door banged open, and a group of teens raced in. By their scent and footfalls, Benuel recognized three of them.

Coltrane burst out. "We found this safety vest in the park out beyond Schrock's Dairy. Could it belong to the missing girl?"

## CHAPTER 15

What was heading through the undergrowth? Thumping feet pounded toward Mari.

Closer and closer.

A lumbering bear? Enraged she'd stumbled too close to its den?

Black bears sometimes attacked. She had to get away.

Mari whirled around and lurched back the way she'd come. She needed help. If a bear had taken Susanna. . .

Blocking off that thought, Mari sped up. But the narrow path tripped her up with bumpy roots, fallen branches, and slippery leaves.

She stubbed her toes. Slid on rotting leaves. Got tangled in vines. Staggered through thin gaps in the trees. Was she even going in the right direction?

Splintering twigs and thundering footfalls kept pace.

The bear was gaining on her.

Lungs burning, she wheezed and panted. She had to keep going. *Faster. Faster.*

Something snatched at her ankle. Encircled it. She jerked her leg to free it. But it only yanked tighter.

Mari semi-turned. A vine. She ripped it away. Spun around and sprinted. Tripped over a root. Sprawled on mushy, dead leaves.

Before she could push herself to her feet, heavy hands pinned her to the ground. Mari writhed, struggled to get away. Her captor smashed her face into the soggy leaves. She couldn't breathe. Twisting her head this way and that, she tried to catch a breath. To dislodge the hands. To free herself.

A kneecap slammed into her back, driving the air from her lungs.

Rough hands tore off her *kapp*. Tears sprang to her eyes as the pins ripped at her hair. She'd lost her precious prayer covering. The man grabbed her bob. Wrenched her head back. A shriek tore through her.

Her abductor stuffed a smelly rag into her open mouth. Tied it so tightly, her head throbbed.

Mari flailed, clawed at the dirt. His knee immobilized her. Then he twisted her arms behind her back until her muscles screamed. In one swift move, he wrapped twine around her wrists, binding them back-to-back.

He stood. Hauled her to her feet. She squirmed, determined to get away. She had to search for Susanna. Had this man kidnapped her too?

Cold metal pressed into the back of Mari's neck. "Stay still or I'll shoot." His low, menacing words sent chills down her spine. Cruelty spiked every word.

Would he really take that chance?

The police and Benuel would hear the shot. Maybe she should sacrifice herself for Susanna.

Ignoring the man's command, Mari pulled harder.

The gun barrel slammed down on her head.

Mari sank into blackness.

# CHAPTER 16

*A*fter the teens burst into the schoolhouse with the vest, Chief Richardson scolded, "You shouldn't have picked it up. Now you've gotten your fingerprints all over it. Drop it on that table." He waved an arm past Benuel's face, indicating the table by the map.

"Sorry. We only wanted to help."

"I can't send my men on a wild goose chase. How do we know it's hers?"

Benuel spoke up. "I can tell."

"Absolutely not. I can't have you fingering the evidence."

"I don't need to—"

The chief interrupted. "We have to follow up any leads we have, no matter how flimsy. And this isn't flimsy."

Benuel longed to check the safety vest. He had no doubt it belonged to Susanna.

"You boys stay right here until I get back," the chief barked. Then he clomped out the door.

Benuel concentrated on Richardson's movements. His car door creaked open. A radio crackled. First, he commanded the squad car supervising the searchers to return to the schoolhouse immediately. Next, he dispatched a K-9 unit to the park.

"We have a safety vest that might be hers," he told them. "I'll send the kid who discovered it out to show the team where he found it."

When Richardson returned, he slammed the schoolhouse door open so hard, everyone jumped. Everyone except Benuel, who'd followed his rapid, insistent steps.

"Which one of you kids found the vest? I'll need you to go with the officers and show them exactly where it was."

Axel's high-pitched voice revealed his fear. "I gotta ride with po-po—? I mean ride with cops? No way, man."

One of his friends clapped him on the shoulder. "Least you ain't gettin' arrested this time."

"I never—"

Sirens split the air as a car roared into the parking lot. Richardson wrenched the door open and hurried out. Although Benuel wanted to listen in, he had something more important to do.

"Coltrane?" Benuel called.

The teen hurried over. "Yeah? You okay?"

Benuel nodded. "Can you bring me the vest?"

"That cop said not to touch it."

"I have to see if it's my daughter's. Please?"

The chief pulled the door open and called to Axel. "You get out here and tell us what you know."

When the door banged shut after Axel, Coltrane hurried to the table and returned, dropping the vest in Benuel's lap. "I used napkins from the snack table to pick it up. Last thing I need is cops taking my fingerprints."

Holding the vest strap between two fingertips, Benuel brought it close to his nose. The ammonia odor overwhelmed him. Susanna had been closer to that stench than the clearing. He didn't want to destroy any fingerprints, so he rotated it slowly as he sniffed, hoping for more clues.

He stopped. An oily patch. He breathed in again, trying to identify the odor. Motor oil.

When he reached the front opening, he detected his daughter's scent. This was hers. His eyes teared up.

Where had she gone? Had she run into the people dumping things in the woods? Did they take her—?

An engine revved outside. Before the police car took off, Richardson would come inside for the vest.

"Put this back," Benuel commanded Coltrane.

Napkins crinkled, and Coltrane whisked the vest away.

"What are you doing over by the table?" Richardson barked at him.

Coltrane didn't answer. He just scurried across the room and slunk into the chair beside Benuel.

"He didn't see me touching the vest," Coltrane whispered. "Gotta get rid of the napkins." Paper ruffled and scrunched in his hands. Then he stuffed the wad into his pocket.

"Thanks for helping." Benuel appreciated Coltrane's assistance. The vest proved Susanna had headed into the woods. How did she end up at the park?

Coltrane leaned over. "Is it your daughter's?"

Benuel nodded. Something else didn't make sense to him. "Why would someone take her to the park? If they kidnapped her, wouldn't they keep her hidden?"

"Sure seems like it."

Chief Richardson loomed over them. "What are you two plotting with your heads bent together like that?"

"Trying to figure out why my daughter's vest smells like ammonia and rotten eggs," Benuel snapped.

"What? You couldn't have smelled that all the way over

here." Then he hesitated. "Or could you?" He took off toward the table.

Coltrane snickered. "He's bending over smelling the vest."

Richardson bit out a curse word. "Very faint. But you're right. She's in more danger than we thought."

What did he mean by that?

Benuel attuned himself to the chief's rapid movements. Latex snapped. He must be pulling on gloves to pick up the vest. A plastic bag rattled. Bagging up the evidence.

Evidence that Susanna had been kidnapped. Evidence that someone had forced her to take off that vest. Or they'd torn it off her.

As Chief Richardson exited, a different thought struck Benuel. Had Susanna taken off the vest and left it for him to find, the way Mari had kicked off her shoes when she'd been kidnapped. Susanna would be smart enough to think of that.

Although Benuel longed to follow that clue, a police dog would search for her. As good as Benuel's senses were, he was no match for a dog's superior skills at following a trail. If Susanna was still in the park, the K-9 team would find her. But if she'd been put in a car, the police would have few clues to her kidnappers.

Benuel had to start searching himself. Not at the park, but in the woods. First for Mari. Then for information about who took Susanna.

*Please, Lord, led me in the right direction to keep my wife and* dochder *safe.*

"But what did the chief mean about Susanna being in greater danger?" Benuel muttered.

Coltrane groaned. "Guess being Amish, you don't know much about making meth. Not that I do. Just from TV. But I've heard that's what it smells like. Did she stumble on a meth lab? Where would she have done that?"

"In the woods. I smelled it at that clearing. I have to follow Susanna's trail. My wife's probably doing that."

Coltrane sucked in a breath. "If they get near a meth house, they could be in real trouble. You don't want to mess with them. Those places usually have spy cams, vicious dogs, and guns. They won't hesitate to shoot."

Benuel froze. Neither Susanna nor Mari would stand a chance against armed criminals. "I have to find out where they've gone. And figure out who has my daughter."

"How would you do that?" Then Coltrane laughed. "Oh, yeah, you'll feel their trails. That was amazing. But, it's too way dangerous, man."

"Can you help me get to the clearing?" Benuel had to rescue Mari before she got trapped. "I'm praying the dogs can track Susanna. But I want to find out who took her in the first place. That information might help if they've taken her somewhere else in a car."

"I can take you down there, but I don't think I should."

"Where's Chief Richardson?"

Coltrane jumped up, went to the door, and returned right away. "He's in his car, waving his arms around. His overhead light's on."

"Can we get down the lane without him seeing us?"

"His back is to us, but we'd be in his rearview mirror." He hesitated. "We might be able to do it if he's distracted and we duck behind the buggy near the door."

Benuel stood and took Coltrane's arm. "Let's go."

# CHAPTER 17

*S*usanna tensed as the boss's grunts reached her ears.
Was he coming here? Did he know Neo had given
her food? She tucked the last of the lukewarm fries into the
folds of her skirt. Balling up the bag and wrappers in her fist,
she shoved them into a crevice between boxes, poking them
back with her forefinger until they didn't show.

She hadn't finished her milkshake. Quickly, she slid it
beside her so it couldn't be seen when the door opened. But
if he stepped inside. . .

*Ach!* The kitten had dragged the container to the other
side of the shed.

What would the boss do if he spotted that—or the
kitten?

Footsteps shuffled closer.

She'd never reach the container in time.

"Not in that one," Junior said. "The girl's in there."

Both men were panting. They must be carrying
something heavy.

Susanna sighed in relief. Maybe they wouldn't come in
here after all.

"Drop her legs," the boss commanded, "and unlock that shed."

*Her legs?* Were they carrying another girl? Had she wandered into the woods too? What was the matter with her that they needed two people to carry her?

"She's a dead weight," the boss grumbled.

Susanna shivered. Her imagination ran wild. Had they killed someone? Were they hiding a dead body? *Maybe they'll kill me too.*

She shook her head. *Neh,* they'd said they'd give her to someone named Duke. Susanna wasn't sure that would be much better. What would he do with her?

*Thud.* Something heavy landed in the shed beside her.

The boss's voice rang out. "Just flop her legs up in there."

Another loud thump.

Susanna winced. That poor girl. Being dumped onto the metal floor like that must have hurt. She hadn't cried out, though.

*Maybe she's gagged like I was.* A gag could be keeping her silent. So could the gun.

*The gun!*

Susanna's hand flew to her temple, where she still felt the pressure of that cold metal against her skin. He'd threatened to kill her if she made any noise.

A horrible sinking feeling snaked through her stomach. Had that girl disobeyed?

If so, maybe she really was dead. "Flop her legs up" sure made it sound that way.

"Junior, get that shed locked up. Hope Duke'll have some use for this one too. She's a bit older than most of his girls."

"She sure is purty."

"Keep yer mind on work."

The shed door slammed. A lock clicked into place.

The men's steps receded into the distance.

Huddling deeper into the blanket, Susanna picked up her handful of fries and tried to warm herself by scrunching her knees to her chest again. It helped a little, but nothing could thaw the iciness around her heart.

She missed *Daed*. What was he doing now? Had he figured out where she'd gone? Would he think to look for Peach at the schoolhouse?

Knowing *Daed*, he'd probably start by tracing her path back to the schoolhouse. But he'd need Mari's help. For the first time in a long while, Susanna was grateful *Daed* had Mari. He'd need her.

Mari had been good for *Daed*. Too good. She did so many things for him that Susanna wanted to do. Right now, she'd gladly give up all those duties to see *Daed*'s face again.

What if he was searching up and down the road for her? Maybe he had taken Peach home first. Poor Peach hadn't eaten.

Suppose *Daed* didn't think to look for her in the woods?

Why had she been so foolish? She'd wanted to upset him and Mari, but she'd ended up hurting herself. And them.

Tears trickled down Susanna's cheeks at the thought of spending the night here instead of in her own bed. Mari often fixed them all cups of hot chocolate before bed. If only Susanna could reach out and pick up her mug, sip the steaming sweetness, dissolve the marshmallow foam on her tongue, and let it slide down to heat her insides.

Instead of a soothing drink of warm chocolatey goodness, Susanna had a handful of cold fries. Still, she ate each one, grateful to have them. Who knew when she'd get anything else to eat?

As she ate, she wondered who they'd locked in the shed beside her. Whoever it was must be lonely and scared. Susanna wanted to reach out and help the girl. *But what can I do when I'm locked in here?*

# CHAPTER 18

*H*ope flickered in Benuel's chest. If they could get past Chief Richardson, they could explore the clearing and find Mari. Benuel wished so much time hadn't passed. What if she'd been hurt?

Coltrane took Benuel's arm and led him to the schoolhouse door. "This'll be the tricky part—going from the light into the dark."

Benuel moved forward eagerly. When they reached the door, Coltrane clutched Benuel's arm, holding him in place.

"Once we get outside, we need to duck. There's a buggy a few feet to our right. It'll be a tight fit, but if we make it, we'll have some good cover."

Gratitude filled Benuel that God had provided this *Englisch* teen to accompany him. Coltrane seemed to be enjoying the intrigue.

Benuel focused single-mindedly on finding Mari. She'd help him pinpoint Susanna's kidnappers. Right now, he prayed for Chief Richardson to be distracted. If the police forbid him to search. . .

He stopped his mind from going there. He'd do whatever it took to reach his love. And to locate his sweet daughter.

"The cop's looking the other way." Coltrane eased the door open.

Thank the Lord, it didn't squeak.

"Now," Coltrane whispered, crouching low.

Benuel followed his lead. They duckwalked several feet. Then Benuel's arm scraped the wood of the schoolhouse.

Coltrane squeezed Benuel's forearm. "We did it," Coltrane murmured. "If we stay behind the buggies, we can make it to that horse shelter." He hesitated. "As long as the cop stays in his car."

Bending over, they moved from buggy to buggy, staying low enough that their heads weren't visible through the windows. They developed a shuffling rhythm. Step, step, stop. Crouch, wait. Listen. Step, step, stop. Repeat. Repeat. Repeat.

Finally, Coltrane whispered, "Short dash to the horse shelter from here. The car light's still on. Let's go."

They rushed across the open area. Benuel stumbled over a stone.

Coltrane stopped to steady him. Glanced over his shoulder. "Sorry," he muttered. "Shoulda been watching better."

Benuel nodded to let the teen know it was all right. He saved his breath for the final push. They sprinted toward the shelter.

"We did it!" Coltrane's low exclamation was filled with relief.

Benuel ran his hand over the boards. "Thank you. You did a great job."

"We're not there yet. We still have the woods. But after we get partway down this hill, nobody can see us from the parking lot."

Together, they negotiated the drop-off, with Coltrane navigating Benuel around divots, tree roots, and rocks. The scent of pine increased, and by the cooler temperature, Benuel could tell they'd reached the woods. The faint odor Coltrane had said belonged to a meth lab drifted Benuel's way.

"It'll be easier to use the lane," Benuel suggested. "If we stay close to the shoulder, we can duck into the trees if a car approaches."

They walked in silence until they reached the clearing.

Now, the stench almost overpowered Benuel. "You smell that?" he asked Coltrane.

"Huh? The trees? Yeah, I like pines." Coltrane guided Benuel off the road to the right.

"Not the trees. The ammonia and—"

Coltrane snapped up straight. "You smell that here? We're near a meth lab?"

"I guess so. I'd say it's several miles in that direction." Benuel pointed northwest of where they stood.

"This isn't a good idea." Coltrane's voice shook.

"Don't worry. We have some backup."

Coltrane let go of Benuel's arm and whipped around. "Where?"

Benuel pointed skyward. "Up there."

The teen snorted.

"Prayer's the best support anyone could have," Benuel assured him.

"I guess." Coltrane didn't sound too certain. "What about human help?"

"We'll have that too." *I hope.* Benuel pulled out his phone.

Coltrane gasped. "You got a phone? Thought Amish didn't have them."

"It's only for emergencies." Even though he always kept

it with him, Benuel never used it for anything else. He concentrated on hitting the correct speed-dial button.

"How can you do that without seeing?" Coltrane asked in amazement.

"I've memorized my screen." Benuel held up a finger for silence. The phone rang and rang. He prayed Ryan would pick up.

A groggy voice answered.

"Did I wake you? It's Benuel Miller."

"Who? Oh, Benuel. Yeah, I was up for thirty-six hours straight. Just finished a case." He groaned. "Don't tell me your sister-in-law escaped again?"

"Not this time." Benuel paused, trying to organize his thoughts. "Susanna's missing. So's Mari."

"Not again."

"I'm following their trail, but there's this odor." Benuel described it. "The teen with me thinks it's a meth house."

"He's probably right," Ryan said wearily. "Don't go near it."

"I have to. I think that's the direction Mari went. Also, they may have kidnapped Susanna and taken her somewhere else. The local police are looking into that, but I need to find Mari."

*And discover the identity of my daughter's captors.* But he didn't tell Ryan that. That would upset the FBI agent, and Benuel needed to ask Ryan a favor.

Ryan growled, "Don't you dare search for them. It's too dangerous."

Benuel stayed silent. He couldn't promise that. As Ryan listed the possible risks and detailed ambushes of agents who'd busted meth labs, Benuel took mental notes. He'd watch for those traps.

"We might not have much time to rescue Mari and find out who took Susanna."

97

After a short hesitation, Ryan said cautiously, "We've been trying to narrow down some meth flowing into Ohio and Maryland from Pennsylvania. We have our eye on a dealer in York, but we haven't discovered his supplier. This might be the link we're looking for."

*Danke*, Lord.

Not only was Benuel glad for Ryan's interest in this area, but Benuel also appreciated Ryan sharing that confidential information. Normally, the FBI agent kept all the details of his life and work to himself. That meant he trusted Benuel with his secrets. A trust Benuel would repay by not divulging anything Ryan said.

Ryan sighed. "Guess I won't be getting any sleep tonight. I'll send a team out. Sit tight until they arrive."

"*Danke.*" Benuel reached for the button to hang up.

"Benuel!" Ryan's hoarse voice barked. "Don't move. I mean it."

But Benuel pressed *End*.

# CHAPTER 19

*M*ari groaned. Flashes of light swam past her eyes. That drumming, rocking car must have driven inside her head. The *whop-whop-whop* ricocheted off her skull bones, setting off a sharp ache behind her eyes.

*Stop*, she tried to moan, but all that came from her throat was a croak. Her tongue had swollen too thick to make the words come out right. And something blocked her mouth, muffling the sound.

As if she'd been spun inside a washer and squeezed through the wringer, her whole body ached.

Cautiously, she opened her eyes, one tiny sliver at a time. Her head swam, and she couldn't focus. Everything blurred.

Exhaustion overtook her. She drifted back into the fog.

After a while, she surfaced again. Memories floated past like clouds. Benuel opened his arms to her. Mari tried to lift hers in return, but they stayed stuck behind her back. She tugged and kicked. But her hands didn't move. Her wrists had lost all feeling.

Benuel's face disappeared into the mist.

*Nooo. . .*

Mari didn't want to lose him. She struggled to open her mouth and beg him to return, but her lips wouldn't part. Folds of cloth bound them together.

Tired of the fighting, Mari lost consciousness again.

SUSANNA WAITED until the men had been gone for some time before calling softly, "Are you all right?"

No answer.

Perhaps the girl hadn't heard her. Susanna didn't want to think about the other, more ominous reason for the girl's silence.

She tried again. Louder this time.

Still no answer.

Desperate, Susanna stood and pounded on the shed wall and screamed, hoping the din would wake her next-door neighbor. Susanna stopped her banging to listen.

Only quietness greeted her.

Susanna beat harder. Screamed louder.

The rasp of the lock startled her. Her arms dropped to her sides. Her whole body grew rigid. What had she done?

They'd kill her.

The door creaked open. Neo stood in the opening, a piece of cloth dangling from one hand.

He'd come to strangle her.

She flattened her back against the cold metal wall behind her.

Neo's eyes looked sad, as if he regretted what he was about to do.

"Please don't," she choked out.

*God help me! Save me! Protect me!*

"I don't wanna do it, but boss said—"

"*Neh*, please. . ." She clasped her hands together as if in prayer.

Neo took a deep breath. Stepped closer. Lifted his arms. The cloth strip stretched between them.

Trembling, Susanna squeezed her eyes shut. *Dear Lord, forgive me for all my sins. Forgive me for how I treated Mari. For the way I acted this morning. For the way I've been acting toward* Daed. . .

Her litany went on and on.

Suddenly, it occurred to her Neo hadn't moved. The cloth hadn't gone around her neck.

She opened one eye to peep at him.

He stood there, rocking from one foot to the other, looking uncertain. "I can't do this." His hands dropped to his sides. The cloth floated to floor.

"*Danke*, oh, thank you. Thank you, Neo." She could hug him. Except he was a stranger. And she didn't go around hugging people.

Neo kicked at the strip of fabric by his feet. "I ain't gonna use that, if'n ya promise not to make no more noise."

A gag? He hadn't meant to strangle her?

A tiny giggle escaped from her lips. "I—I thought"—she gestured to the dirty rag. "Never mind." After Neo's kindness, she didn't want to insult him by telling him she'd believed he was a killer.

"I'll be quiet. I promise." She made the motion of zipping her lips.

His breath came out in a long exhale. "Good. But Boss'll kill me if ya makes a sound."

He reached in his pocket and pulled out a short rope.

"What's that for?" Susanna kept her voice barely above a whisper.

Neo held his wrists together and gestured toward them with his chin.

She gulped. "You're going to tie my hands together?" She slid them behind her back. Her fingers scratched nervously at the shed wall. "I won't bang on the wall again."

He stared at her for a long, uncomfortable minute. "Ya better not." He tossed the rope on the floor.

"*Ach*, thank you, Neo. Thank you."

With a nod, he turned to go.

"Wait," she whispered. "Tell me about the girl in the other shed. Is she all right?"

"Don't know."

"Is there any way I can help her? Is she hurt?"

Neo shrugged. "I ain't seen her. Boss clonked her with his gun."

"Oh, no. She does need help. Neo, please let me take care of her."

Rubbing a knuckle across his lower lip, Neo stared at her.

"I won't make any noise. We can't let her die." Susanna had no idea how to save a dying girl, but she had to try.

Neo glanced toward the blackened windows of the house, just visible through the open shed door, then back at her. Without saying a word, he waved toward the door.

"Just a sec." Susanna tied the blanket around her neck. She bent, scrambled for the kitten, scooped it in her arms.

Then she picked up the rope, the rag, and the rest of her milkshake. The kitten wriggled, and she almost dropped everything.

He reached out, grabbed the milkshake, and motioned for her to go out the door first. After he locked it behind him, he fumbled through his key ring.

Susanna's heart jumped in her chest when he unlocked the other shed. How badly hurt was this girl? Would she be able to help?

Neo eased the door open, and Susanna stepped inside. She gasped and stopped dead.

# CHAPTER 20

hen Benuel hung up the phone after talking to Ryan, he let out a pent-up breath. The FBI would take care of the meth house. Meanwhile, Benuel would rescue Mari.

*Rescue?* Why had that word popped into his mind?

Up until now, he'd assumed Mari had gone into the woods to hunt for Susanna. He'd been picturing her moving ahead, healthy and strong. Now other possibilities flooded his mind. Suppose she'd started following the trail and had gotten hurt. She could be lying in the trees somewhere. Or—

His mind didn't want to go there, but suppose she'd discovered Susanna and had been taken by the kidnappers too? Maybe he was headed in the totally wrong direction.

*God, please direct my path.*

His confusion cleared. He'd check for Mari's footprints to see if he could figure out where she'd gone. If he couldn't, he'd leave the meth house to the FBI and ask Coltrane to drive him to the park to search.

"You okay?" Coltrane asked with concern.

Benuel pulled his lips into a wan smile. "Just thinking."

"Your friend gonna help?"

His friend? Oh, Ryan. Benuel had been so busy concentrating on Mari's whereabouts, he'd forgotten about Ryan.

"*Jah.* He'll send a team to check out the meth house."

"A team?"

"Some FBI agents."

"The FBI?" Coltrane's voice rose in pitch, and he stepped back. "You're with the FBI? And just pretending to be Amish? But you're blind? Or is that fake too? It's a good cover."

Benuel laughed. "*Neh*, I can't see. I'm really Amish. And I'm not with the FBI." Not that they hadn't asked him to join after Mari's kidnapping.

"What? Then who? How?" Coltrane stared at Benuel in confusion. Finally, he stammered out a coherent question. "Why do you have the FBI on speed dial? You an undercover cop?"

"*Neh*, just an ordinary Amish man. Look, I need to find my wife. If you help me find her prints, I'll tell you more about it."

Coltrane led Benuel over to the spot where Mari had been when he left her, then they both squatted down, and Benuel ran practiced hands over the ground until he'd identified one of Mari's prints.

"See this. These are the prints we're looking for."

"Wow. That barely shows. All I saw was mushy leaves and pine needles."

"But they're crushed here. And the ground is slightly lower. Feel it."

"You're right." Coltrane acted as excited as a child who'd been given an unexpected present. "There's another."

Benuel smiled. He loved the teen's enthusiasm. "Think

you can follow them to see where they lead?" It would save time if Coltrane found where Mari went. She could have paced, backtracked, walked in circles.

As Coltrane walked, Benuel told him about Mari's kidnapping on their wedding day, how the FBI got involved, and how his sharpened senses helped him save Mari from being arrested.

"That's, like, awesome."

Benuel smiled. "*Jah*, God is awesome."

"Not God. I meant you and all the stuff you did."

"I couldn't have done it without God."

"You really believe that, don't you?"

"For sure and certain."

Benuel tried to explain. "Faith in God is like breathing. You never wonder if there'll be enough air for your next breath. The air is in you and around you and always there. And it keeps you alive. It's the same with God. Except God does so much more than just keep you alive. He gives you a reason for living."

"Wish I could believe like that." Coltrane sounded wistful.

"You can. Try praying. Just talk to God. Be honest."

"He wouldn't want to listen to me."

"Try it. You might be surprised. Reading the Bible and going to church help too."

"I used to go to Sunday School when I was little." Coltrane's voice came from far away. Not only because he'd moved closer to the woods, but more because he seemed lost in thought.

Benuel stopped talking to let the boy process his memories.

"Hey!" Coltrane shouted. "They go into the woods right here. Look! Um, I mean, come and feel it."

Excitement pounded in Benuel's chest as Coltrane led

him to the narrow opening between two trees. Benuel sank to his knees, uncaring of the dampness soaking his pants legs. They were already filthy.

Coltrane guided Benuel's hand to the indentation.

*Jah*, it was Mari's print. He stretched his hand out eagerly. There was the next one. *Danke*, Lord!

Benuel turned to Coltrane. "I'm going to follow this trail. I need you to stay here and wait for the FBI."

"The FBI?" Coltrane's voice squeaked. "I—I can't do that. Why can't I go with you? Or I could follow the tracks. I can do it faster."

"I'm depending on you. There are things I'll need to do." *If anything happens to me, it'll be God's will.* Benuel didn't want Coltrane to run into any dangers near the meth house. The teen wasn't ready to meet God.

Benuel clasped Coltrane's arm again. Ordinarily, Benuel might not have done this, but he felt God compelling him to finish his conversation with Coltrane. "Before I go. . ."

Praying his words would find a receptive heart, Benuel spoke the words the Lord gave him. "Church, the Bible, and prayer are all important and helpful, but if you really want to get right with God, you need to ask for forgiveness. And forgive everyone. Including those you're holding a grudge against."

Coltrane spoke through tears. "How did you know?"

"I didn't. God led me to say that."

A hiccupping sob revealed God had a reason for those words.

"Once you've made things right with others, surrender your heart to the Lord and commit to following His will. That'll keep you on the right path in life."

"Thank you," Coltrane gasped out.

"Don't thank me. Thank God."

With those final words, Benuel crawled between the trees to follow his beloved's footprints, praying he'd find her at the end of the trail.

# CHAPTER 21

*S*usanna clapped a hand over her mouth so she wouldn't scream.

Mari lay still and silent on the shed floor.

Teary-eyed, Susanna stared down at her stepmother. All the love she'd had for Mari while *Daed* courted her flooded back. "I-Is she dead?"

"I don't think so." Neo studied Mari. "Look, her chest is fluttering."

How could he tell that in the dark? Susanna's eyes were too misty to focus. She sank to the floor and set a hand on Mari's chest. Her breath was shallow, her chest barely moved.

"I gotta go. They find out I done this and——" He slid a hand across his throat like a knife.

"Thank you, Neo. Thank you so much."

"Yeah." Neo's voice was gruff, but the kindness underneath shone through.

As the door shut and locked behind him, Susanna studied Mari. Susanna had been so focused on Mari's breathing, she hadn't noticed the gag in her stepmother's mouth. Susanna scooted around in the tight space to get behind Mari's back.

With gentle pushes, Susanna rolled Mari onto her side. Her stepmother's hands were tied behind her. The men had tossed her into the shed on her back, trapping her hands beneath her. How that must have hurt!

Susanna worked at the knots, breaking fingernails as she struggled to work the rope free. When the bindings fell off, Susanna rubbed Mari's hands to get the blood flowing through them. The rope had bitten into Mari's wrists, leaving her skin raw. Poor Mari! Susanna moved the top arm to the front of Mari's body, but the other arm was still pinned behind her.

Quickly, Susanna moved up and untied the gag. Then she rolled Mari to the opposite side in slow motion, praying she wasn't hurting her. Finally, she freed Mari's arm. Her stepmother groaned.

She must be in pain, but the sound was reassuring. She was alive. Maybe she was even coming around.

Susanna took off the blanket Neo had given her and covered her stepmother. Then she tiptoed around Mari's body, almost stepping on Snowball's tail. The kitten had curled up by Mari's feet. After positioning herself with her back to the cartons, Susanna lifted Mari's head onto her lap. She stroked Mari's *strubbly* hair. What had happened to her *kapp*?

Unless it was hidden in the deepest shadows, the *kapp* wasn't in the darkened shed. She must have lost it when Junior and the boss grabbed her. How had she gotten captured? What had they done to her? And why was she here?

*Was Mari looking for me?*

Guilt filled Susanna. Mari could have been killed. *And it would all be my fault.*

"I'm so sorry," she whispered as she undid the hair netting around Mari's disarrayed bob and gently removed the hairpins, setting the hair free from the messy bun.

Then Susanna combed her fingers carefully through Mari's tangled locks, avoiding the huge bump she'd discovered on the back of Mari's head.

A lump as large as the one choking Susanna's throat.

*If I hadn't been so selfish. . . If I hadn't been so greedy—wanting all my father's love. . . If I'd been willing to share. . .*

Mari never would have been hurt. We'd never have been locked in this shed.

*Dear Lord, forgive me. Please heal Mari.*

Susanna's well-trained fingers form a fresh bob, twisting the side locks tightly, flipping the hair over her hands, making a bun, inserting the hairpins in the right places. Then she wrapped the netting around it. All she needed now was the *kapp.*

The *kapp* Mari had lost because of Susanna's *hochmut.*

When she finished, Susanna placed Mari's head back in her lap. What if she never got better?

*If only I could take back everything I did to hurt Mari. And* Daed.

Mari groaned. Susanna smoothed a hand over Mari's hair, brushed gentle fingers down her cheeks.

"Benuel?" Mari croaked.

"*Neh*, it's Susanna.

Mari's eyes fluttered open. "Susanna? Thank the good Lord, we found you." Then her lids drooped.

The words pierced Susanna's heart. They both had been looking for her, despite her behavior that morning. She'd been convinced they wouldn't care or even notice if she left, but that wasn't true. Deep down, she'd always known they loved her, but she'd let herself be led astray.

Once again, Mari opened her eyes. This time, they stayed open.

"Is it really you, Susanna? Or am I dreaming?"

"It's really me." Susanna hung her head. "*Ach*, Mari, I'm so sorry for how I treated you. I was jealous of the time you spent with *Daed*."

When she said her father's name, she ached to see him. "Where is he?"

"I don't know. We split up. He followed the pony cart tracks because Peach came home without you. I followed your footprints."

"Peach went home?"

"*Jah*, she broke free of her reins. Oh, and everyone in the community is out searching for you. I wish I could let them know where you are."

That news humbled Susanna even more. She'd caused so much trouble for all of them. "I'm so sorry for all this. Can you forgive me?"

"Of course. If you'll forgive me for not realizing you needed more time with your *daed*." Mari struggled to sit up. "*Ooo. . .* I'm dizzy." She winced as she lifted a hand to her head.

A puzzled look crossed her face. "I thought he messed up my hair."

"He did." Susanna bit her lip. "I fixed your bob, but I couldn't find your *kapp*."

Tears filled her eyes. "That man yanked it off. It must be somewhere in the woods. I wish I could cover my head."

Susanna reached for the rag that had served as a gag. "Would this work?"

Mari wrinkled her nose. "*Ach*, Susanna." Then she

laughed. "Can you tie it on me? God will know my heart's in the right place."

*Jah*, Susanna had no doubt about that. Mari's heart had always been in the right place. If only Susanna had realized it sooner.

# CHAPTER 22

*B*enuel felt his way along the trail, grateful for Mari's clear footprints. Often, she'd stepped close to the side of the path, leaving Susanna's steps clear in the center.

He marked his passage with small piles of stones or pebbles every ten to twelve feet to make the route easy for the FBI to follow. Crawling along on all fours was slow going, and he had to brush the ground in front of his knees each time he moved forward. He cleared the path before him, then placed his hands down cautiously, and crept ahead.

The wetness seeping into the fabric of his pants legs chilled him. The night grew colder, and he wished he'd worn a heavier coat.

He traveled a long time before he reached an area that worried him. Mari's prints had been obscured by larger ones. The wearer had a heavy tread, and the shape of the heel seemed to belong to a cowboy boot. From the way the prints were scattered, a scuffle had taken place here.

After that point, Mari had made no more prints.

That worried Benuel. Where had Mari gone?

He circled the area twice, even checking the ground under the bushes. On his second round, his hand encountered stiff fabric. Familiar stiff fabric. He lifted it and examined it. His heart dropped like a stone thrown into a pond, sending off ripples of fear in its wake.

*Nooo. . .* What had happened here?

*Ouch!* Something pricked him. He ran his fingers cautiously along the band. She hadn't removed any of the pins. Strands of hair clung to the inside, some still wrapped around the pins.

*Oh, dear Lord, no! Please no! Protect her wherever she is!*

Benuel scrunched his face, trying to ward off the frightening images swirling through his mind. Someone had torn this *kapp* from his wife's head. Someone had hurt Mari here. More than hurt her. Shamed and humiliated her. Someone had made a mockery of her faith. And trampled it into the ground.

For her hair to be ripped out like this, her attacker had been strong. Strong enough to fight off Mari's attempts to hold on to her *kapp*. Knowing his wife, she wouldn't have let go easily. Her prayer covering showed her devotion to God.

He turned the *kapp* over and over in his hands wishing it would yield a clue to who had done this.

And Benuel had only one guess as to Mari's location. That man must have carried her off. Benuel's heart contracted. Had she been dead or alive?

He should have been here with her. He'd been so intent on following pony cart tracks he'd left his darling wife behind to be accosted by strangers. Dangerous, desperate criminals who'd stop at nothing to guard their illegal business, according to Ryan's stories.

Leaves crunched in the distance. Several twigs snapped. The sharp crack of breaking wood alerted Benuel to a presence in the woods. Most people wouldn't have picked up that sound. Not yet. But Benuel had. Someone or something was headed his way.

A slight shuffling. The crinkle of crisp, dead leaves. The squish of soggy ground sinking under heavy boots.

Definitely not an animal.

He suspected it might be the person who'd made these prints. Benuel needed to conceal himself in case this person—a man, judging by the weight he put on his boots —had been the one who'd taken Mari. And possibly Susanna.

The dried undergrowth and dead vines provided no cover. Benuel belly-crawled under a spruce whose branches swept the ground. The needles prickled him, but the tree provided good cover.

Someone stepped into the clearing. From the air vibrations, Benuel sensed the man's semi-crouched stance, his arm partially extended. Did he have a gun? It wouldn't be a hunting rifle. His arm wasn't out far enough. It must be a handgun. This man wasn't an innocent hunter. He intended to hunt a different kind of game—human beings.

Benuel's heart stuttered.

*Please, Lord, I beg you, please let Susanna or Mari still be alive.*

The man spun in a circle, disturbing the leaves. Benuel held his breath. Would he be spotted under the spruce? The branches had felt full when he'd checked, but maybe a gap he'd missed exposed him to view.

"Junior," the man snarled. "Where'd you see the intruder?"

*Are there two of them?* Benuel tensed.

A tinny voice answered. "The same place ya found that there girl."

Benuel relaxed a little. A phone.

"Check the monitor," the man ordered. "Tell me where he went."

115

"Don't see him, boss. It was crawling. Coulda been some animal."

"You'd better be sure."

The man made one last circle of the area, then hurried back in the direction he'd come.

After waiting for him to move far enough away, Benuel turned and crawled after him. No need to get close. The man lumbered like a groggy bear, dazed by spring sunshine and unsteady after waking from winter hibernation, leaving a trail of broken branches, trampled twigs, and deep dents in the soggy ground.

Benuel regretted not having someone with him. They could race down this path after that man instead of crawling along. But the footprints and disturbed brush made him easy to follow.

The stench grew stronger, making Benuel sick to his stomach. A loud whirr of fan blades—one of the signs Ryan mentioned—signaled caution. Benuel must be approaching the house.

Nearby, animals made weird noises. Not growling exactly. A lower, almost choking, menacing sound. Dogs? Benuel felt sick. Maybe dogs who'd had their vocal cords cut.

Both Ryan and Coltrane had warned him of dogs. Ryan had said they often didn't feed the dogs so they'd attack. Benuel prayed they were all caged.

*Whop-whop-whop.* A helicopter chopped the air, swooping low, turning in slow, lazy circles overhead.

# CHAPTER 23

*a* loud chopping sound shook the shed.

Susanna sat bolt upright. "What's that?"

"Sounds like a helicopter." Mari's eyes kept drifting shut.

"It's so close. And it's not flying over. It's circling."

Mari's lips barely formed the word "police."

"Please, Mari, stay awake." Susanna shook Mari's shoulder. "If it's the police, maybe they'll rescue us."

"I don't think there's any place to land around here." Disappointment colored Mari's words, but she made an effort to straighten up.

Outside, the boss screamed. "Neo, set the trash piles on fire. Junior, dump lighter fluid around the fence. Use the flamethrower to torch it. Create a huge cloud of smoke so they can't see us."

Susanna clasped her hands together in a prayer. "Please, Lord, if it's the police, let someone find us."

THE SCREECHED COMMANDS reached Benuel's ears. They were setting the place on fire. So far, he'd identified three men—Junior, Neo, and the one from the clearing, who seemed to be the leader. Were there more?

Did they have Mari here? How could he find out? If they'd killed her, maybe fire would destroy the evidence.

*Please, Lord, direct me. help me find my wife.*

The crackling grew louder as flames whooshed into the sky. Benuel choked on smoke and lighter fluid fumes. The dogs went crazy, jumping at the fence.

Overhead, the helicopter continued to circle, but its path widened. It shook the trees overhead each time it passed. The blades were deafening.

"Open the gate, you fool," the leader shouted into the throbbing air. "Don't set that on fire. We have to get out." He sounded panicked.

*A gate?* Benuel had to find that gate and get inside. But how?

"Get over here and help me load the truck," the man boomed. "We have to save what we can."

"What about the sheds?" a boy asked.

His voice high with desperation, he sounded like a teen.

"Leave them. We can't save everything. Just grab the stuff we can sell."

"What we gonna do with them dogs?"

Benuel identified him as the other man on the phone —Junior.

"Press the button to let them out. They can take care of any coppers in the woods."

*The dogs?* Benuel had to escape. Most of the trees around him were evergreens. None of them would hold his weight. If only he could see.

*Dear God, please help me. Show me where to go.*

All around him, animals scrambled away from the smoke

and approaching flames. Birds flapped high over the treetops. Benuel shuffled along from tree after tree.

Finally, an oak. The lowest branch was so high off the ground, he had to shinny up to it. It had been years since he'd climbed a tree. His legs were still in biting distance when the metal gate clanged open and a rush of rabid dogs raced out.

Susanna panicked as the air filled with smoke. "They're setting everything on fire. And they're leaving us here."

Mari forced her eyes open. She had to do something, but what? "What's in these cartons? Is there anything in them to put out fires?"

"The other shed had soda. Can that put them out?" Susanna sounded doubtful.

Hadn't Mari read somewhere about soda being used like a fire extinguisher? "I think so. Do we have any in here?"

Susanna stood and headed for the far end of the shed. Mari checked near her.

"*Jah!*" Susanna crowed. "Here are some cartons. Can you help me get them down?"

Mari's head ached, and she felt nauseous. Her arm muscles burned, but she joined Susanna in maneuvering several boxes from the stack.

The shed grew hotter. The fire must be getting nearer. Mari didn't want Susanna to panic, but they might be overcome by heat in this metal box long before the flames reached them.

As THE DOGS charged toward him, Benuel flung an arm over the lowest branch and dangled there.

The pack raced past, their muted barks echoing around him. They must be chasing the fleeing animals.

*Danke*, Lord!

Benuel dropped to the ground. Now, he only had to face three—or more—criminals with guns and raging fire to find Mari. He had two names to give the police. He hadn't heard the leader's name.

His cell phone buzzed. He pulled it from his pocket.

"What do you think you're doing?"

Ryan. His fury radiated through the phone.

"I'm near the house. They're burning everything. Except the merchandise."

"I know." *The chopper's keeping us informed.*

"But I don't know where Mari is." Benuel tried to keep his voice from shaking. "The smoke's getting bad."

"A team's on the way in, and the fire department's en route, but I'm not sure either of them'll make it before the place goes up in smoke. If Mari's inside. . ."

Ryan didn't finish his sentence, but Benuel didn't need him to.

METAL SCRAPED AGAINST THE LOCK. It clicked.

"It's Neo." Susanna raced to the door. "He's letting us out. We can get away."

"Who?"

Mari didn't want to stamp out Susanna's excitement, but if those men let both of them out, it'd probably be to kill them.

Still, she couldn't tamp down a tiny bud of hope at the scrape of the lock being lifted from the padlock.

When it was partway up, a loud slap rang out. The shank slid back into place.

"Leave that be."

"But the girls. . ." Neo's words ended in a gurgle.

"Junior's choking him." Susanna banged on the door. "Leave Neo alone."

"Boss," Junior shouted, "this guy's trying to let those girls out."

"Don't you dare. Drag him over here. We're leaving."

A jangle of keys hit the door and slid to the ground.

Susanna crumpled into a heap inside the shed and covered her face with her hands. "Neo almost opened the door. But now there's no way out."

Mari sat beside her and wrapped an arm around her. "Let's pray." But even she felt it was hopeless.

*THE SHED.* They had girls locked in the shed. Would Mari be there too?

The truck engine roared. Gravel sprayed Benuel as it zipped by. He prayed they hadn't seen him. Exhaust from the truck and smoke from the fire choked him.

Benuel coughed and pulled his shirt up to cover his nose and mouth. Now he just had to find the gate where the truck had exited. He didn't have time for caution. No feeling along the ground for obstacles on his hands and knees.

Grabbing a dead tree branch from the ground, he swept it along in front of him until he found gravel. Then he turned and rushed up the driveway. Flames surrounded him on all sides. Hissing and spitting and throwing sparks.

The chopper headed off after the truck.

"Mari?" he called, praying for an answer.

"Benuel," she yelled back.

"*Daed*," Susanna's joyous scream sent Benuel's spirits soaring. She was here. The safety vest must have been a decoy.

"We're in the second shed."

"I'm coming." Benuel longed to run toward them, but he couldn't risk falling and hurting himself. "Keep talking so I can find my way."

He brushed the stick along the ground impatiently.

Susanna chattered on. "Neo almost unlocked it. I can't wait to see you. I'm so sorry for causing so much trouble and being mean to you and Mari. I told Mari I was jealous about how much time you two spend together and I don't get to do anything with you anymore. . ."

Benuel had reached the shed door. It was hot enough to burn his hand. He used the stick to dislodge the padlock and yank open the door.

As it creaked open, Susanna flew into his arms. "Will you forgive me?"

"Of course."

Mari joined them in a group hug. Then she gasped. "We're surrounded by fire. Even the grass in front of the gate is burning."

Susanna let go of him. "Soda," she said.

Mari followed her into the shed. She returned and handed him a soda bottle.

She took his arm. "I think if you shake it up, it works better."

Susanna clung to his arm, and they raced toward the opening.

"Now," Mari yelled and unscrewed her bottle. They squirted it in front of them, and wherever the soda spattered, the flames died.

"Run before it catches fire again," Susanna shouted, and

they all raced through the narrow opening between the wall of flames.

They didn't stop running until they'd gone far down the gravel path toward approaching fire sirens.

~

A FEW HOURS LATER, after all three of them had been checked by EMTs and debriefed by the FBI and local police, they made their way home. As soon as they got inside, Benuel opened his arms and embraced his wife and *dochder*.

He blinked back tears. It was hard to believe they'd made it out of there.

"You know, I had to rescue you from a shed on our wedding morning," he said to Mari. "I hope you're not going to make a habit of getting locked in sheds or outhouses and expecting me to rescue you."

Mari laughed until tears rolled down her cheeks. She snuggled closer. "I'll try never to do that again. Although I have to admit, seeing your face when the shed doors open reminds me how much I love you and how special you are to me. And it makes me grateful to God that He brought you into my life."

Benuel nodded. "*Jah*, and it makes me realize how precious life is, and that we shouldn't take each other for granted."

She nodded. "We don't know how much time we have left, so we need to love each other."

Susanna hugged them both hard. "*Jah*, we do! I'm so glad you found me and that you're my parents, *Daed* and. . ." Her voice broke on the words "and *Mamm*."

123

# THANK YOU FOR READING THIS NOVELLA

I'm grateful you chose it. I hope you enjoyed traveling to Lancaster County Amish country, and I pray the story uplifted and blessed you.

**If you enjoyed this story, I hope you'll read my Amish novels.**

The links below will take you to my pages:

Website: http://www.racheljgood.com

Amazon author page: https://www.amazon.com/Rachel-J-Good/e/B019DWF4FG

Facebook: https://www.facebook.com/racheljgoodnovels

Thank you ever so much!

**Rachel**

P.S. If you'd enjoy learning more about the Amish, you're welcome to join my private Facebook group, the Hitching Post:

https://www.facebook.com/groups/196506777789849/

And if you haven't already, you can sign up for my newsletter at http://bit.ly/1qwci4Q

# ABOUT THE AUTHOR

## RACHEL. J. GOOD

*USA Today* bestselling author Rachel J. Good writes life-changing, heart-tugging novels of faith, hope, and forgiveness. She grew up near Lancaster County, Pennsylvania, the setting for her Amish novels. Striving to be as authentic as possible, she spends time with her Amish friends, doing chores on their farm and attending family events.

Rachel is the author of several award-winning, bestselling Amish series in print or forthcoming – *Love & Promises*, *Sisters & Friends*, *Unexpected Amish Blessings*, and *Surprised by Love*, along with two books in *Hearts of Amish Country* – as well as many anthologies, including *Amish Christmas Twins* and *Christmas at the Amish Bakeshop* with Shelley Shepard Gray and Loree Lough. She is also the coauthor of the *Prayerful Author Journey: Inspirational Weekly Planner*.

Rachel hosts the Hitching Post, an online site where she shares Amish information and her book research. She also enjoys meeting readers in person and speaks regularly at book events, schools, libraries, churches, book clubs, and conferences across the country. Find out more about her at: http://www.racheljgood.com

Connect with Rachel

Hitching Post
Newsletter sign-up

Facebook
Goodreads
Pinterest
BookBub
Instagram

# ALSO BY RACHEL J. GOOD

## HAVE YOU READ THEM ALL?

## SISTERS & FRIENDS series

### *Change of Heart*

When her younger sister goes wild during *Rumschpringa* and dates an *Englischer*, Lydia Esh teams up with his older brother to break up the couple. But she doesn't count on falling for an *Englischer* herself. Will Lydia stay true to her faith if it means giving up the man she loves?

### *Buried Secrets*

Emma Esh has recovered physically from the accident that almost claimed her life, but she has no memory of the year before the accident, so she has no idea why her sister tries to keep her from falling in love with their next-door neighbor Sam Troyer. But an unexpected visit from an old boyfriend and the gradual return of her memory tears Emma's life and romance apart.

### *Gift from Above*

Sarah Esh's peaceful life is torn apart when a parachutist crash-lands on her family farm and begs her to keep his presence secret because his life's in danger. That promise tangles her in a web of deceit that endangers innocent people, ruins her best friend's reputation, and tears apart the Amish community. Sarah must confess and repair the damage she's done, but how can she admit the truth to Jakob Zook, knowing it will end their relationship?

### Big-City Amish

After Abner Lapp's betrayal and his choice to leave the Amish community, Rebecca Zook tries to forget him, but how can she ignore his mother's plea to watch his four young brothers during her cancer treatments in New York City, even if it means being around Abner? Rebecca's tender heart won't allow her to ignore him when he's hurting, but she can't let herself fall for him again, especially when he's not right with God.

## LOVE & PROMISES series

### The Amish Teacher's Gift

A teacher at the Amish school for children with special needs, Ada Rupp struggles to balance her job with caring for her seven orphaned siblings. She has no time to date, but she'll do anything in her power to help her young student, Nathan Yoder, and his grieving widowed father.

### The Amish Midwife's Secret

When Amish midwife Leah Stoltzfus insists on using herbal remedies for her patients, sparks fly between her and the new *Englischer* doctor, Kyle Miller. In more ways than one. Can they overcome their differences to rescue a pregnant teen and save her unborn baby?

### The Amish Widow's Rescue

After Grace Fisher's husband dies unexpectedly, her neighbor, the reclusive Elijah Beiler, offers to help with her animals and household repairs just to be neighborly. He has no intention of getting entangled with the pregnant widow or her children; he's been hurt enough in the past. But he hasn't counted on Grace's young son, who's determined they need a new daddy.

~

## UNEXPECTED AMISH BLESSINGS series

### *His Unexpected Amish Twins*

When Micah Miller becomes the guardian of his twin niece and nephew after their parents are killed in a buggy accident, he's grateful for Hope Graber, owner of a horse therapy farm, who helps all three of them all deal with their grief. Hope makes them smile again and wins a place in Micah's heart. But will his deep-seated fears and Hope's close partnership with her *Englisch* trainer keep them apart?

### *His Pretend Amish Bride*

Priscilla Ebersol has no chance of marriage after her boyfriend's humiliating rejection ruins her reputation, but after she helps an Amish camel farmer in a nearby town and she's mistaken for his wife, Priscilla's matchmaking *mamm* sees this as the perfect opportunity. Unfortunately, her meddling might drive the couple apart instead of together.

### *His Accidental Amish Family*

Following a buggy accident, Anna Flaud is told she'll never walk again. She refuses to accept that and spends years recovering, and she's also working toward becoming a foster parent. Then she's offered a chance to fulfill her dearest wish—motherhood—by adopting three siblings with special needs. But it comes with strings attached: she needs a husband. Her exercise therapist, Levi King, would be perfect for the role except Levi can't trust himself to care for one child, let along three.

∼

## SURPRISED BY LOVE series

### *Unexpected Amish Proposal*

After Fern Blauch loses her market stall, Gideon Hartzler offers to share his stand with her, but once they start working together, will her rival in business end up as a rival for her heart?

### *Unexpected Amish Courtship*

Isaac Lantz, who trains Labrador retrievers as guide dogs, is enamored with Sovilla Mast, who sells homemade dog food and treats. Gaining a dog's affection is easy, but bashful Isaac has no idea how to win the heart of the woman he loves.

### *Unexpected Amish Christmas*

To help himself recover after a buggy accident, Jeremiah Zook pens inspirational letters to grieving families mentioned in the Amish newspaper. Moved by the letter he's sent, Keturah Esch corresponds with him. Little does she know, Jeremiah has a nearby market stand. When he shows interest in her, she rebuffs him because her heart belongs to the anonymous letter writer. A Christmas gift accompanied by a letter might just hold the key to both their hearts' desires.

### *Amish Marriage of Convenience*

When widower Stephen Lapp moves his five children from New York State to Lancaster County, Pennsylvania, his only plan is to buy his family's farm stand. But on Stephen's first trip to the market, his brave act of kindness nearly ends in catastrophe—until strong-willed Nettie Hartzler saves him—and makes an impression he can't forget. Nettie has no interest in getting involved with any man. But when Nettie runs into serious money worries and Stephen proposes a marriage of convenience, she's distressed and conflicted. She's come to know Stephen's gentle heart and generous soul, but will he marry her if she reveals her dark past?

### *Her Pretend Amish Boyfriend*

Noah Riehl has dark secrets in his past that prevent him from marrying a faith-centered Amish girl like Caroline Hartzler. But when she needs a fake boyfriend to discourage a persistent suitor, who won't take no for an answer, he agrees to rescue her. But will his kindness lead him into the very relationship he's vowed to avoid?

### *Dating an Amish Flirt*

Everyone accuses Rachel Glick of being a flirt because she's caused several breakups and broke many hearts, but she only wants to spend time with her brother's friends after his death. Josh Yoder wants to help the grieving family, and God seems to be leading him to Rachel. But with her history of breaking hearts, is she the right choice?

### *Missing Her Amish Boyfriend*

Anna Mary Zook is struggling to cope with her new job at the market and care for her five younger siblings as Mamm spirals into another depression. Abe King longs to be there for her, but he can't leave his aging father to run their New York state farm alone. Can Abe and Anna Mary find a way to be together?

≈

## ANTHOLOGIES

***Amish Christmas Twins***, ***Christmas at the Amish Bakeshop***, ***Amish Christmas Kinner*** (with Shelley Shepard Gray and Loree Lough)

***Amish Christmas Miracles***, ***More Amish Christmas Miracles***, ***Amish Spring Romance*** (with Jennifer Beckstrand, Jennifer Spredemann, and others)

***Amish Across America*** (free; with multiple authors)

***Amish Christmas Cookie Tours*** (with Mindy Steele and Jennifer Beckstrand)

***Love's Truest Hope*** (with Mary Alford and Laura V. Hilton)

***Love's Thankful Heart***, ***Plain Everyday Heroes***, ***Love's Christmas Blessings***

(with Laura V. Hilton and/or Thomas Nye)

∼

## NOVELLAS

***Amish Christmas Treasure***, ***Amish Mistletoe & Miracles***, ***Amish Wedding Day Revenge***, ***Amish Twin Trouble***, ***Missing Amish Daughter***, ***Amish Secret Identity***, ***Amish Thanksgiving Strangers***

∼

## OTHER TITLES

***Amish Quilts Coloring Book*** (regular and large-print versions)

*Prayerful Author Journey: Inspirational Weekly Planner*

*Hearts Reunited* in *Hearts of Amish Country series*

*Love's Secret Identity* in *Hearts of Amish Country series*

**Check for more Rachel J. Good titles here.**

Made in the USA
Las Vegas, NV
14 July 2023